HEART OF RESURRECTION

BONNIE ELIZABETH

My Big Fat Orange Cat Publishing

Heart of Resurrection
My Big Fat Orange Cat
Fantasy 2023

Copyright 2023
Bonnie Elizabeth Koenig

Cover image Copyright © "blackmoon979", "Zuzule" | Deposit Photo

Cover Design Copyright © Bonnie Koenig

My Big Fat Orange Cat Publishing
MyBigFatOrangeCat.com

All rights reserved. No part of this book may be reproduced without written permission of the copyright owner.

ISBN 978-1-953363-21-3 trade paperback

Chapter One

I loved Jewel Island and the people there despite the fact that I seemed to be a magnet for troublesome ghosts.

I loved having magic. I continued to work on accepting myself for who I was—fat, divorced, and someone who had struggled to find her place in life. On Jewel, I felt on top of the world. That is, until Grant N. Arwen, mage psychologist arrived on the island.

Grant had been called there to do an assessment on my co-worker, Jack. Recently, Jack had been not quite possessed—that requires spirit magic which Jack doesn't have—but under an influential spell. They'd gotten him to put a sleep spell on the coffee in the office to attempt to kidnap me and allow another powerful mage to take over my body. Fortunately, I'd had some protection so that that spell had failed. The mages who had done this to Jack were smart and devious, which meant Grant would be on the island working with him for some time.

The day Grant walked into the office was one I wouldn't forget easily. I'd been settling back in to work. It was the first day I hadn't seen a single dragon-fly, (which was not actually a misspelling but the way we differentiated them from their namesake insects) which suggested, given how attached they'd become to me, that they were gone for the season. Dragon-flies were not the insects that most people thought of, but tiny dragons that appeared around enclaves on varying schedules. Ours had appeared just over a month ago and had hung around during the time when Jack had been influenced. They had nothing to do with that, though. They had in, fact, protected me from the same fate.

I'd become fond of the dragon-flies, enjoying their antics, so now that they were gone, I felt a bit down. I stopped in at our grocer which sat on the corner of the main road on the island for a Frappuccino, hoping to drown my sorrows in caffeine and sugar.

I was proud of myself for not hiding that I wanted one, not trying to deny myself because of what people would think about the fat woman drinking a sugary drink.

At forty, divorced, childless, and looking for a job I'd become increasingly disgusted by the fact that it seemed as if employers were just looking for reasons not to hire me. My weight was merely one reason. I'd not had the energy to shame myself into being smaller and, instead, had let go, surprised at how often I was welcomed.

My sisters didn't care. Their kids didn't care. In fact, when I babysat my sister Charlotte's children, they said they loved my softness, as they called it. Their acceptance had given me a reason to be proud.

I enjoyed walking. I loved to swim, though I had rarely done it when I was younger because I was too embarrassed to put on a suit. However, I'd needed to do things for me so I swam at the indoor pool—I mean, even before moving to Jewel, I lived in Michigan. You can't exactly swim outside year around. I'd even started dancing.

Slowly, I realized the only reason I cared about being fat was the fact that not all chairs or spaces were large enough to accommodate me. It dawned on me, that was their problem not mine. I didn't get to that point all on my own. I can thank the internet for many of those insights. I started to accept my body and my life, even if I was still unemployed and living in my older sister's basement and the feelings of failure hadn't completely gone away.

After those months of self-image struggle, I got the job on Jewel and during my training, I'd come to realize that the part of myself I was still most ashamed of was my weight. I also learned that the more I accepted myself, the stronger my magic would be. Apparently, I'd done well because I had strong spirit and fire magic. My earth magic was average, but I struggled with water and air, though I could protect myself from an attack using either of those elements if I had to.

At any rate, I'd been working as an accountant on Jewel for over seven months. I'd managed to avoid being killed not once, but twice. I had friends, even a couple of really good friends, and I was settling into my job.

I was coming to terms with the fact that Jewel Island didn't appear on any maps and yet we got mail regularly and we also had phone and internet service. If it was raining, umbrellas appeared in large urns near the doors of all buildings, including homes. Chairs were always perfect for my size and comfortable. The one restaurant changed at every meal so no one felt as if they were eating the same old thing again, unless, of course, they wanted to.

While I could tell my sisters I worked on Jewel Island, no one ever asked me about why they couldn't find it. That struck me as odd at first, but Bernice, the mayor and one of the people who taught magic to me, said it was normal.

People only found the island, or any of the magical enclaves, if they were actually coming into their magic.

Of course, non-magical people could visit if invited, though I had no idea how that worked. My overly developed imagination pictured an invisible engraved invitation on the guest's forehead that only the island would see.

Jewel Accounting, where I worked, was in a ranch house that hugged the edge of a low cliff overlooking Lake Michigan. The backside was nearly all windows and I had a spectacular view from the main waiting area as well as my office. Jack, the bookkeeper I worked with, had an equally marvelous view from his office.

Jack was working quietly at his desk when I arrived with my Frappuccino, the smells heavenly to my nose. Because the island was magic, it was the perfect temperature and tasted equally heavenly on my tongue.

I knew Jack was working on some month end items for some of the businesses. We each did some of the work, though I double checked Jack's. I did so because it was my job, not because he needed to have someone look it over. It would be an understatement to say Jack was a perfectionist. I knew he double and triple checked himself. I don't think I ever found a single error on his part.

I'd barely settled in to do my own work, my fancy, sugary coffee still warm on my desk, when the front bell dinged. I stood up slowly, when I didn't hear Jack's voice immediately calling out to our visitor. He was clearly involved in what he was doing, leaving me to play receptionist. I didn't mind. I liked the people on the island.

Standing in our waiting area, beside the small reception desk we had just in case we ever hired a receptionist, was a tall, dark-haired man. His hair was short and had a hint of a curl where it draped slightly over the tops of his ears. His skin was dark beige and his nose long and narrow against chiseled cheekbones.

With his coloring, I'd have expected him to have dark eyes, but instead they were a startling blue. And kind. Even a bit sexy, as was the half smile he gave when he looked at me.

I'm old enough to be past the idea of love at first sight, but this man…well this man did it for me. I noticed the long thin fingers which could have belonged to a concert pianist and wondered what they'd feel like running across my skin. I wanted to know what the moist lips felt like against mine.

My belly fluttered with desire and curiosity and while those eyes were startlingly blue and oh so very kind, they seemed to see through someone and into their soul. I didn't need to offer a porn movie at first meeting.

"Can I help you?" I asked, hoping my voice didn't shake. I tried to imagine myself acting like my friend, Ian. He would have sashayed over and leaned against the desk, sticking out one hip. He'd probably tell me to stick my breasts out. But I'm old enough and my breasts large enough, that would probably have looked ridiculous.

"I'm Grant Arwen. I'm here for Jack." His voice was soft, soothing. If he asked me to stand on my head, I'd have done it. And that was without the attraction. I wondered if he used magic to make people comfortable, although from what I'd learned, that sort of suggestion was forbidden. Besides, my arms hadn't tingled the way they normally did when someone used magic around me.

I wished the little dragon-flies that had been flitting around for a month were still there to distract me. It took a moment for me to nod and then head back down the hall to Jack's office. I wondered if Grant were watching me walk. Uncharacteristically, I wondered if he found my butt too big. I wished, suddenly, that I were slender and pretty and about five or six years younger.

Grant was probably close to my age, but it would have been nice to be the younger woman.

Jack was working quietly at his desk, not noticing I was there. I cleared my throat. He practically jumped.

"Grant Arwen is here for you," I said. The room was silent. Even our HVAC was off for a change. With the huge windows it's almost always running, either the air conditioning or the heat and sometimes both on the same day.

Jack's face paled.

I remembered Ian telling me that Grant had been on the island before. I guess Mindy, a waitress up at Derry's, had had some issues that she'd worked through with him. If it were me, I'd never get over my issues just so I could keep talking to him. Of course, that would have meant I'd have to talk about my issues, which was not easy for me, though I had a feeling that Grant would have made it possible.

I backed away from the door, not daring to look back at Grant, certain that all he saw was a far too large butt covered in black slacks that probably didn't fit as well as I had thought they did this morning. I should never have had that Frappuccino.

Back in my office, I glared at the mug on my desk. I hadn't needed the calories. I hadn't really needed the sweet flavor, no matter that it had cheered me up after the dragon-flies had disappeared. I just hadn't needed it and now those calories were probably expanding my butt and thighs even as we spoke.

Breathing in, I was uncomfortably aware of the tightness of my bra. Before it had always felt comfortable, thanks to David's wonderful sizing magic. Now, though, I was too aware of it, wanted it to be larger, though it had been comfortable moments before.

I shook my head, hoping to push those thoughts out of my mind and get to work.

Numbers didn't hold me, though. I kept thinking about Grant.

I'd gotten through about three items when I heard the bell ring and then Jack's soft steps back down the hall. No doubt Grant had only stayed to set up a meeting with Jack. I wondered where they'd meet and decided that it was probably at the library, where there were extra rooms for any sort of need. Either that or the hospital.

I went back to working with a spreadsheet I had open. The HVAC clicked on, cool air, the day's bright blue skies were warming the interior of the building. I'd nearly finished when I heard something outside my office. It didn't sound like Jack moving around. I knew his sounds.

I glanced up and noticed a shadow at the doorway. It wasn't even shaped like Jack.

I pushed myself up from my chair, which, now that I thought about it, hadn't felt as comfortable as it normally did. It had felt almost ordinary, pushing a little too hard on the sides of my thighs. Looking out my door I could see the main entrance.

I saw a woman standing there, but for just an instant, before she winked out of existence. Ice flowed down my back as I realized the gray hair and the slightly pudgy shape belonged to Sharon, the former mayor. She'd died when she'd failed to catch some magic she'd tried to murder me with and I'd deflected it back to her. That had been nearly seven months ago. Recently, her spirit had been active, but I thought we had managed to put her to rest or perhaps even banish her. Apparently, I was wrong.

My spirit magic allowed me to see ghosts. Normally,

they looked like regular people. While they might fade away, they didn't normally pop out like turning off a television set. Maybe this was a new thing.

The room got colder, and not just from the chill inside me. It was the cold of a spirit nearby, though if one were that close and that cold, I ought to have been able to see them.

The temperature dropped even further until my teeth chattered.

While it's disconcerting to see dead people, at least when I saw them, I knew where they were. I could tell if they were kindly disposed or not. Now I could only feel the chill. And that was worse. I had no idea what Sharon wanted. Before, she'd been trying to steal my magic. Given that she wasn't visible to me, I worried she'd finally succeeded and I hadn't even noticed.

Chapter Two

A month ago, I hadn't even known a spirit could try and steal my magic the way Sharon's had tried to do. I shivered in the chill, not even thinking about calling out to Jack. No use exposing him to another spirit. For all I knew—and I knew far too little—having been influenced once by another mage could make it possible for Sharon to possess him, though normally, only those of us with spirit magic were susceptible.

I dug in, my fingers reaching back to grasp the doorframe of my office, feeling the hardness of the wood that made up the building. I focused on all the magic hiding in my generous thighs and my ample belly. I pictured magic in the folds of my fat, because for me, my biggest shame was being a fat woman. I had lots of other things to be ashamed about but my weight had always just felt like the thing that caused all the other issues.

I mean, yeah I was divorced, but at least if I were small no one could say it was because of my body. Ditto the no job before I'd come to Jewel, and so on and so on.

But because I was able to overcome my body shame

and accept my body, I had magic. I focused on all the good things my body had done for me. It allowed me to walk all over the island. It got me up in the morning. It stored my magical abilities.

I realized that earlier this morning, I'd been judging myself in a way I hadn't in a long time. I couldn't have said why. Perhaps Sharon was trying to undermine me, though she didn't know the reasons I had come into my magic. Maybe I was just lusting enough after Grant and seeking to blame my body for any lack of attraction.

As I focused, Sharon appeared in front of me, hovering. She wasn't quite as solid as most ghosts when I saw them. Normally they look as solid as real people, but I could see shadows through Sharon, though she wasn't quite fully transparent.

"Be gone," I said, putting for my will into it.

Sharon faded out. She didn't quite pop the way I thought she should. But then again, I hadn't had much training in spirit magic. Lucas, another mage with strong spirit magic, was working on remedying that, but we were both healing from over-extending ourselves the week before. We'd only had two sessions so far.

I wondered why I hadn't been able to see Sharon the entire time she'd been in the building. Spirits weren't normally able to hide from me. I needed to talk to Lucas.

I passed Jack's door but it was closed. I imagined him working frantically at the numbers, checking and double checking. He probably even checked my figures but I couldn't help that. I didn't knock. It wasn't like we had to check in on each other. During tax season we hadn't, though now that the office wasn't quite so busy we both usually called out if we were leaving.

Stepping outside, I was greeted by the sounds of the

surf slapping against the island. A gull screamed from somewhere distant.

There are no cars on Jewel. Normally people walked or used scooters or golf carts, with walking the preference for everyone except those who lived the furthest and those with a disability. Kara, for instance, rode around on her mobility scooter. Deanna just used her wheelchair which seemed to move easier on the island than those I had seen on the mainland. Probably thanks to the magic.

I knew Dirk and Bill often rode horses into town. When I'd gotten to know them, I'd learned that they turned the horses out in a field on the other side of the docks. There were no fences but the horses knew to wait.

Nearly all the animals on the island were like my cats. They had their own magic. If their people needed to get somewhere, the horse would probably appear where needed, just as Peony and Tulip had a tendency to do. When I'd been in the hospital, Peony would show up snoozing next to me though there was no way an ordinary cat could have gotten out of my condo. I hadn't been there long enough to worry about the cats going without food so no one had checked on them.

That was a mistake I wouldn't make again. The litter box had been a mess and one of them, probably Tulip, had used one of my houseplants instead of the box.

Normally I appreciated the silence and being alone with the sound of the surf. Today, it felt sort of ominous, as if I might be the only person around, though I knew I wasn't.

I looked longingly up the hill at the B&B. I wanted to go chat with Ian. He'd calm me down, have some wisdom that would make me feel better.

While I headed up to the B&B, I knew in my heart I needed to talk to Lucas not Ian. Ian's a slave to gossip and loves being in the know so I knew he'd be disappointed that I'd want to talk to Lucas rather than him. Well, that and he was my friend and he'd want to be helpful.

Of course, last time Ian had been helpful he'd overextended his magic and could have died if he weren't what was called "The Innkeeper." In fact, he still wasn't quite himself, his sashay was a little less pronounced and he didn't bounce across a room quite as quickly.

The B&B is a big old Victorian. The building was done in pink and green and the small garden in the front accentuated both colors, from the pink blooms on the flowers to the greenery that surrounded them. It looked, if I dared say it, magical.

And it was.

It wasn't just that Ian had magic and ran the place. The B&B itself was magical. If someone arrived and needed a room, the building would create one. On busy mornings, such as when Ian served Eggs Benedict, the dining room expanded, adding more tables for everyone who wanted to be served.

When Ian had overextended himself, it had been the B&B which supported him. I wasn't quite sure how the bond between Ian and the building worked. While it had protected him, it would not have protected anyone else in quite the same way.

The bell on the door—which was probably superfluous as Ian just knew when there were guests, both on the island and entering the building—hadn't even stopped ringing after I entered before Ian sashayed out of the kitchen.

He had workers to cook and to clean up, but no matter when I arrived, it seemed like he'd appear from the dining room and the kitchen area. Asking him about it did no good. Ian had given me an enigmatic look, an exaggerated shrug, and laughed.

I watch far too many horror movies and read too many horror novels, so of course when that happened, I had an image of a long cord running out of Ian's body plugged into an outlet over an ordinary kitchen stove, while Ian sat alone in a chair, his head hanging down like a marionette. The image stayed with me, though it was rather laughable. Ian had hugged me, rescued me, and had nearly given up his life for the people on the island. He'd dragged himself through a deep depression not long after, and was finally himself again, mostly. He was as human as I was, though he might have an odd bond with a building.

"I'm actually hoping to see Lucas," I told him, clearly apologetic that I hadn't come just to see him. I breathed in the smell of coffee that always permeated the building. I considered asking for a cup, knowing Ian would definitely get me one.

"I'll give him a call," Ian said. He walked over, with somewhat less than his usual swagger, to a small writing desk that served as the reception desk and picked up a phone I'd never noticed before. It was an old black thing with a rotary dial. Ian didn't look old enough to have used one before coming to the island.

He dialed only a single number and waited.

"Holly is here to see you," Ian said. He listened for a moment and hung up.

"Lucas will be down in a minute," he told me, gesturing me into the dining room.

"Thanks," I said. "I thought I saw Sharon earlier. I'm not sure what's going on. She wasn't as solid as usual…and for a time I couldn't see her at all."

Ian frowned. He'd been involved in helping rescue me from Sharon, both when she'd tried to murder me when she'd been alive and then again when she'd been attempting to get another mage to possess me after she'd died. Everyone had loved Sharon and I hated that I had been the one to kill her, even if inadvertently and in the only manner the island would allow. No one blamed me but me. It was something I was going to have to live with though it was difficult.

I heard the thump of Lucas' feet on the stairs. He was the roundest person I have ever seen. He's not a big man, nor particularly fat. He's just round. From his face to his belly, though his belly wasn't that large, just round.

"What's up?" Lucas asked.

I repeated what I'd just told Ian about Sharon. Ian moved off to get us tea while we talked. I asked for coffee, which made Ian laugh and shake his head as he went off to grab our drinks.

"Did you feel her?" Lucas asked.

"When I couldn't see her, I knew she was there because the room was icy cold, like spirit cold. I had to focus on my magic before I could see where she was, and even then, she didn't look as solid as ghosts normally do."

I hated thinking that Sharon could come upon me unaware. Lucas had started working with me to train my spirit abilities, but I knew I had a lot left to learn.

"Was there anything new in the environment?" Lucas asked.

I shook my head. "I mean, Grant Arwen came in and talked to Jack, but that's all. Grant's been checked out, right?"

After what had happened with people arriving on the island just a few weeks ago, I wasn't taking any chances with strangers. I mean, the whole reason they were on the island was to help us make sure we were all safe, but it was natural to distrust strangers. Even if they were overwhelmingly handsome.

"If Grant gave you the look," Ian said, arriving back

carrying a tray, his hip pushed out, tightening the front of the black pants he wore, "I'd have forgotten all my magic, too."

He set down the tea pot and a mug for Lucas. He put a hot mug of coffee before me. He looked at us, as if waiting to be invited to sit, but neither of us asked him.

I wanted to. Ian had been my rock. But sometimes Lucas asked me incredibly personal stuff and I wasn't sure I wanted to share all of that with Ian. Heck, I didn't want to share it with Lucas, but he insisted it would help him train me.

After a moment, Ian sashayed off as if he didn't have a care in the world. I thought, from the set of his shoulders, that he was a bit hurt, which bothered me. I should have asked him to stay. I'd apologize later.

"Everyone is getting vetted before coming to the island," Lucas said. "We'll be doing that for several months, at least until we know for certain that Damien is gone."

I shuddered at the thought that he might not be.

"This isn't about Damien, is it?" I asked keeping my voice low. "He couldn't have done this?"

"I'm as certain as I can be that he's gone," Lucas said. "Several other spirit mages have gone to Far Haven and found no trace. There's one who does medium work and no spirit has been able to find him at all. He's gone. But because of what he's done, we're taking extra precautions around Jewel, more like those that are done for Far Haven."

Far Haven was the enclave that housed a prison for mages accused of magical crimes. Damien had been held there, but he'd found a spirit mage to help him possess another mage, and finally, when all else failed, Damien had allowed his body to die. Lucas had banished his spirit with my help. I'd thought dealing with Damien and his helpers was over, but apparently not.

"Even so," Lucas said, "I don't like Sharon being involved. And the fact that you couldn't completely see her. Give me your hand and open your mind."

I drew in a breath and let it out before placing my hand in Lucas's. He was going to search through my memories. Given my reaction to Grant, I wasn't sure I wanted to have that happen. For the moment, I was glad I hadn't asked Ian to stay.

Chapter Three

I know everyone has insecurities, but as a fat woman, I tended to be more insecure than most about my looks. I didn't normally think about them. Normally, I was fine. But when it came to attraction, well certain cultural norms had been drilled into me at a young age. And then, when my ex had left me for a younger, thinner woman and started the family we'd been planning almost immediately, well that had been a blow.

Sitting in the B&B, the long, narrow, pine plank flooring solid beneath my feet, the rounded chair fitting my butt perfectly, and the aroma of coffee and spicy tea tantalizing my nose, those things seemed petty and silly. I was here. I had magic. What more did I want?

I tried to blank my mind and not think of Grant Arwen and his beautiful smile, but it was a tough thing to do. Lucas was going to pick up on that attraction. My face heated at what he might think.

Slowly, my mind cleared. Lucas moved a little as he held my hand. Pressure built on my forehead, though it wasn't bad. If Lucas had pressed his fingers against that spot it would have felt much the same, though I knew this was all energy and magic.

I breathed in deeply, calming my heart, trying not to be too embarrassed. The pressure eased and I opened my eyes.

Lucas nodded.

"I can't say for certain that Sharon did anything. Your magic is weaker though. I sensed something around Grant, which I think you need to clear on your own," Lucas said. "Now isn't the time to be distracted and doubting yourself. The more you accept yourself, the more magic you have."

Suddenly, I felt like a cartoon character with a light-bulb going on. Talk about an a-ha moment. I'd been worried about my looks, about my body because of my attraction to Grant Arwen.

"Could Sharon's spirit have somehow sensed my weakness?" I asked quietly, hoping I was wrong.

Lucas nodded grimly. "I had a sense that Sharon wasn't completely gone, but seeing what went on in your office, I now know for certain. Spirits absolutely know when magic weakens. Someone like Sharon would exploit it. The good news, if there is any, is that it's clear that Damien isn't easily able to access the island, even if he is still around… and I don't think he is."

That probably should have made me feel better, but deep down I felt like a failure. I had let a man, a good looking man to be certain, make me doubt myself and my body. I had let someone else's perception of me interfere with my ability to accept who I was—*all* of who I was.

"Then I guess I need to get back to self-acceptance," I said quietly, not sure how to go about doing that.

Lucas nodded. "We all have pitfalls around those things that we've felt shame over in the past. Things come up.

Don't let it get to you. It's just kind of bad timing for it to happen now."

I had to agree. I walked out of the B&B, wishing I could have run to Ian and talked to him, but he hadn't come out of the kitchen again. I hadn't even finished the coffee he had made for me. Another thing to feel badly about.

The day might have been lovely, the light breeze cooling the warmth from the sun just enough to make it feel perfect. I didn't notice a single cloud in the sky, not even a puffy white one. The air smelled fresh and clear and the sound of waves should have been soothing, but instead it reminded me of all my failures.

I walked up the steps to the accounting office only to find the door locked. I frowned. It was unlike Jack to leave in the middle of the day. I fumbled around for my key, unlocked the door, and went inside.

Jack's office door was still closed. I knocked.

Waited.

No answer.

Frowning, I turned the knob. The room was a mess. Papers were everywhere on the floor.

Carefully, I stepped inside, wondering if I should back out and call Xavier. But I was aware of the fact that I didn't know my coworker very well, giggling a little as I realized that meant I didn't know Jack.

Giggling over silly things and laughter at something I shouldn't laugh at told me I was pretty stressed about what had happened. I wondered if he'd been gone before I left. But I hadn't locked the door. Someone else had.

I hoped that someone had been Jack.

The corner of the desk held a splotch of dark red, so faint I would have missed it if I hadn't been searching for something to tell me what had happened. When I saw that, I did back out of the room.

I set my bag down on the reception desk and called the police department, talking to Rose, the old woman who answered the phones and worked at the front desk. She was slow with a head bob that never seemed to stop and always made me a little worried that her head would eventually fall off. However, I'd learned in the last month that Rose was a powerful mage and while she didn't move quickly, she got the job done. When she said she'd have Xavier over immediately, I knew I wouldn't have long to wait.

Biting my lip as I sat down at the front desk, I worried that someone had hurt Jack. If he was still influenced and we hadn't noticed, it was equally possible that he'd hurt someone else, though I didn't think we had any appointments that day. This was not a good time for me to be questioning my worth or having to deal with the shame of being a fat woman.

The office was silent, the refrigerator off, the HVAC off. From where I sat I didn't even get the faint sound of the waves against the beach. The only sound was my breath and the squeak of the chair that moved slightly every time I twitched.

Remembering my training, I focused on my breath. In that light meditative state, I reminded myself of all the wonderful things my body did for me. I remembered that there were men who found me attractive just exactly as I was. If Grant Arwen wasn't one of them, then I didn't need him. And of course, my mental discussion went on about whether want and need were really all that different because I certainly wanted him.

The door blew open and my face flamed. I'd been so

involved with my internal discussion that Xavier's entrance surprised me.

"Lucas called just before you did. He's concerned that your powers are diminished. And then you called because Jack is gone?" Xavier looked at me. He's fairly tall and very thin. His skin is as dark a brown as any I'd seen. His clipped short hair even allowed a peek at the skin on his skull.

Chief of Police, Xavier was a good cop. He was smart and fair. Sometimes he intimidated me, but he'd always been kind when I needed help. Even when I felt foolish for calling.

"I went to see Lucas because I felt Sharon, but didn't see her. When I finally did, she wasn't as clear as ghosts normally are. It worried me that I wasn't able to sense her the normal way. When I came back from talking to Lucas, the front door was locked. Jack's office door was closed. I knocked, but he didn't answer. That wasn't normal, so I opened the door and the room was a mess. If that wasn't strange enough, there's a reddish-brown spot on the corner of the desk," I said. I would leave it to Xavier to decide if it were blood.

I watched as Xavier walked over to Jack's office. I noted the way his back stiffened when he looked in. Jack's need for order and tidiness was well-known by just about everyone on the island. People weren't supposed to speculate on where someone's power came from but I'd always gotten the impression that everyone assumed Jack's power came from his compulsive need to keep things tidy and to have everything anyone could possibly need at hand.

My arms tingled. Xavier was using magic. The tingling faded quickly. Xavier stepped through the door and into Jack's office.

I got up and followed, though I waited outside. I made

sure not to touch the doorframe, just in case, though I doubted anything would be found. I rubbed my arms, waiting and watching.

Xavier looked down at the desk, knelt by the papers reading what was written. He sighed.

My arms tingled again. This time it lasted longer. Xavier turned around and around in the room. Then he stopped. The tingling stopped.

"Did you look at the papers?" he asked me.

I shook my head.

"Come and see if you see anything that looks unusual."

I walked in. Squatting down but not touching the papers, I noted that several were printed spreadsheets. I recognized one for the B&B charges which Jack always checked over. Another was for David's clothing store. Instead of charges, it was a profit and loss statement for two months ago.

"The B&B charges are current, so that's normal. David's clothing store's statement isn't," I said. "I don't know why Jack would have had that on hand to toss around unless he randomly printed things to make a mess."

"Or someone else did," Xavier said.

I stood up and slipped out, careful not to step on any of the papers. I hated that our client's private information was there for all to see.

"Did you sense anyone else there with your magic?" I asked when I got to the doorway. He might not answer, but I had to ask.

Xavier shook his head. "Did you?"

"I've never had the sort of magic that tells me if someone has been around. I can't even say for certain if a spirit has been around, not unless I saw them."

"Who was here this morning? You and Jack? Any customers?"

I went through the fact that Grant Arwen had come in for Jack earlier. Xavier made a note.

"There's not too much blood on the desk. Maybe he got a paper cut?" I could tell by his tone he didn't believe it. Neither did I.

For the second time in a month, I wondered what had happened to my coworker. The last time his connection to me had caused him to be targeted. I worried that the same might be true of today's disappearance.

Chapter Four

Last time Jack had disappeared, he'd been influenced by a mage with spirit magic. Jack hadn't been in control of himself and had put sleep spells on our coffee pods. Then he'd taken the ferry and left the island. I hadn't had a clue what had happened to him until later, when he'd called me. Jack had sounded scared.

Because of the depth of the influence, Jack was supposed to see Grant Arwen to determine if he was completely clear. The mage who had likely put the spell on him and forced Jack to do these things had been arrested and was being held in a facility far from Jewel Island, but that didn't mean Jack was completely free of the spells.

As I understood it, a powerful spirit or spirit mage who found a way to influence—or in the case of another mage who had spirit magic, posses—another person, could leave behind suggestions. The most subtle of those suggestions could last for years and change the way the person behaved. While none of us had noticed anything and Lucas hadn't detected any lingering spells, it would take an expert on psychology to really delve into Jack's mind. That's where Grant came in.

Now that Grant was here, Jack had disappeared. The question was whether or not his disappearance had been voluntary. The spot that might have been blood concerned me.

"If it was a long-lasting suggestion to avoid Grant, could Jack have been trying to fight it?" I asked, thinking about the blood and the scattering of papers around the room.

"An interesting suggestion," Xavier said, nodding. "Not impossible. While I don't sense anyone, that could have been wiped if they had magic. My concern is that there's someone here we don't know about just like last time. You haven't seen Ian have you?"

I nodded. "When I saw Lucas. Ian didn't mention anyone, and I know he's been working on his connection and making sure no one else slips onto the island," I said.

Last month, two mages had managed to hide their arrival on the island from the Innkeeper. Supposedly, that wasn't possible, but there were a lot of things that weren't possible in theory that had happened on the island. Ian had been working to make sure it didn't happen again. If he'd been able to get a fix on who was on Jewel and where they were, we might have caught them sooner.

"I hope this doesn't have anything to do with Damien, still," Xavier said. "He might be gone, but Sharon is clearly still around."

"Lucas hasn't been able to find Damien's spirit at all. We're pretty sure he's gone," I said. "And I'm not sure what Sharon can do."

Xavier had his hand on the doorknob. "Don't underestimate Damien's ability to hide. He'd have sent Sharon out first because he wouldn't want people to notice him. While

I tend to think he is gone, we can't completely rule it out. He didn't need to have magic in life to be a powerful spirit in death and his will to live and to keep on living made him a formidable foe."

I was left with that thought and no response. I didn't want to think about the types of forbidden spells that Damien had found. Almost as if someone was guiding him. And maybe that person was still on the island.

Which gave me another idea. I grabbed my things and locked up the office for the second time that day. I'd clean up Jack's office later on just because we have confidential information on the businesses that others shouldn't see. I figured if Xavier wanted to send Carl over for more mundane forensics, he would. The buildings typically let in a police officer, even if the doors are locked.

The day was still clear and bright though I still felt as if I had my own personal gray cloud hanging over me. When I got to the B&B, Ian didn't come running out to meet me as he normally did.

I waited in the little entry area. I could have gone into the dining room and sat down at one of the tables, or I could have headed to the right and sat in the little parlor that looked out over the front porch. Instead, I chose to stand, hoping to get an idea from Ian about what was going on and how annoyed he was with me for not sharing what had happened during my meeting with Lucas.

Listening to the soft music that piped through the building, I let my mind wander. I wanted Ian to be okay with not being involved in what I told Lucas. I wanted to apologize to him for not speaking up. I could explain that I was nervous around Lucas and didn't know what he'd planned. Hopefully, the fact that I'd returned would go a long way to making up with my friend.

I started to get annoyed. I mean, Ian normally wanted

to hear everything. He understood that he couldn't be involved in certain aspects of people's lives even if they confided in him later. Really, the fact that he wasn't there was odd.

I walked into the dining room and called out his name.

I heard nothing. Not even a cook or dish washer.

Socrates, the black cat that hung out around the place, wandered into the dining room. He looked at me and howled. Not a happy to see you howl but more of a distressed howl, or at least that's how I heard it.

That brought Edie out to the front. She's older and thin and helps out at the B&B sometimes.

"What's going on?" she asked. She looked at me and then at Socrates as if the cat could actually talk.

I mean, it could, sometimes, but not in cat form.

"I came back to talk to Ian," I said.

Edie frowned. "He was in the kitchen and came out through the dining room, I thought. But that was before you arrived. I would have thought he was in the parlor?"

Edie stepped out and looked into the parlor, as if I could have missed someone sitting in one of the wingback chairs or the green sofa that sat beneath the window. Edie lowered her head to see if perhaps Ian had fallen to the floor.

She stepped into the parlor and even looked behind the sofa, lest he be playing a particularly odd game of hide and seek.

Shaking her head, Edie frowned. "I only heard the door once…although I could have missed it."

"What about the back?" I asked.

"He didn't go through the kitchen. I suppose he could have created a back door to leave through the main part of the building, but why would he?"

"He could have been mad at me," I said. "I talked to Lucas earlier and I know he wanted to listen in…"

Edie waved a hand. "Ian's not that petty. I know you two are friends and share a lot but he's good about respecting privacy. He'd just ply you with food and drink until you told him later."

I laughed because that was much more the Ian I knew.

"Where could he be?"

"I'm calling Xavier," Edie said. "I don't like what's been going on here and Ian has been in the thick of it."

I pulled out my cell phone and tried Ian's, but I didn't hold out much hope. At each ring he didn't answer, my heart sank a bit further.

Edie disappeared into the kitchen. I glanced over at the black phone on the little desk and decided to try calling Ian from there. That way if he were upset with me, he wouldn't know it was me.

I picked it up, looking at my cell phone for his number and carefully dialed it. It rang once and then someone picked up.

"Hello?" the voice was male, but not Ian's.

"I'm trying to reach Ian," I said.

"The Innkeeper is not here right now," the voice said. It almost mimicked Ian's voice but it had a sort of tinny hollow quality that didn't belong.

"I need to find him," I said.

"So does the Inn." And the connection was cut.

I frowned looking at the phone.

Turning, I found Socrates sitting by the front door, staring at me. His golden eyes were large in his black face. He didn't move as I stepped towards him.

"Do you know where he is?" I asked.

Socrates gave his head a shake as if something had touched his ears, which was probably as close to a negative as a cat could give. That really bothered me. The cats were powerful and they knew the island. If the B&B, assuming that had been the building on the phone, and the cats didn't know where Ian was, there was a problem.

My heart rate sped up. The island was now down two people.

I started to sweat, waiting for Edie to return. While I did so, I worried she would disappear, too, and I'd be left alone on Jewel to try and find the others when I didn't even have all my powers.

Fortunately, it didn't take her long to return. Moments later, Lucas came down the stairs and looked at us.

"Xavier called. He said Ian's missing?"

I nodded.

"I'll try to connect to the B&B spirit and see what it says," he said.

"I used the black phone on the desk and tried Ian's cell phone in case he just didn't want to talk to me," I said. "I got a voice that sounded like Ian but more hollow and a bit on the tinny side. It said the Innkeeper wasn't available. I told it I needed to find him and it said the Inn needed to do so, too, and hung up."

Lucas frowned. "An interesting way of communicating, but I suspect the B&B knows that you and Ian are close, so it was able to reach you. Your connection to spirit probably helped..." he paused looking around. "Still let me try."

"Socrates also doesn't know where he is," I said.

Lucas looked at the cat.

"Now that's bad."

He moved slowly into the dining room and settled at a table, closing his eyes. I wondered if I should join him, but it seemed like too much work to go over there.

Around me the B&B started to creak and groan. The

air felt heavy and thick and far too warm though the day was comfortable outside.

Even after Lucas looked up and opened his eyes, the feeling didn't change.

"I'm not sure we should stay in here," he said. "The place is not pleased that no one knows where Ian is. It's going to start getting very cranky."

He moved faster than I would have believed and so did Edie. I followed. Even Socrates leaped through the door and somehow managed to land in the garden instead of on the porch. None of the cats were curled beneath the little Japanese maple that created a focal point there. Socrates took off down the road to parts unknown. He didn't turn to wait for me, so I waited with Lucas and Edie just on the other side of the gate to the B&B.

Something had happened and it wasn't good.

Chapter Five

The beautiful green paint on the outside of the Victorian B&B began to darken to something closer to a forest green. The pink dulled to a grayish color. The budding low, red Japanese maple got darker, almost black in color, and looked like something out of a Halloween card. Even the air seemed cooler and the fresh smell of the day turned slightly rotten, as if there was a landfill nearby.

The sound of a golf cart reached me. Turning, I watched Xavier arrive, his expression concerned.

"Bernice called. The island is more than a little distressed," he said.

"How could Ian just disappear and the island not know anything?" I asked.

Xavier frowned. "It's happened before. An Innkeeper was spelled and taken off the island, hidden from it. He couldn't be killed here. There haven't been any boats. Not only are both Bernice and Gretchen aware of when one comes, I've stationed Kara in the little boat house to physically watch for one. She's got a wonderful attention span and can sit and watch the waves for hours."

Kara was bit older than me. She mostly rode around in a mobility scooter, though I knew she had a wheelchair as well. I often came across her when I left my condo. She'd settle herself on the beach and watch the waves. She said she was a night owl, didn't sleep much, and she worked as an IT consultant during the late hours.

I didn't know her well, but I knew that she was well thought of in the community, though she tended to keep to a small circle of friends. I suppose I could say the same about me. It was just that our circles didn't much overlap.

"Can Bernice tell if Ian was taken off the island?" Lucas asked quietly.

"She doesn't think so," Xavier said. "The island would know if he'd died so there's some powerful magic going on."

Both men glanced at me. I swallowed. I hoped that they didn't think I had something to do with it.

"Who could do it?" I asked, my voice hoarse and low. The wind took that moment to come up and practically blew away my words, but clearly both knew what I was saying.

"Damien could have," Xavier said. "And he could have made us forget. I doubt Sharon could have and Damien is gone."

"So far as I can tell," Lucas said. "It *is* possible I'm wrong and he's still here."

"Could he have hidden himself in someone? Maybe put a kernel of his spirit in someone like Jack?" I asked. It was probably ridiculous. I did watch too many horror movies. You'd think that living on an island where magic was the norm, I'd stop watching those darned things.

"Unlikely," Lucas said. "I'd have felt the pull of something on his spirit and I haven't found anything. Besides, Jack doesn't have spirit magic and even a mage as powerful as Damien would have had a hard time possessing someone without even a little spirit magic."

"What about Grant Arwen?" I asked. "He's new on the island. I know he was checked out but he's the only thing different from yesterday."

I hated to point fingers at him, but he was seductive. Ian had felt it, mentioned it to me weeks before Grant had arrived on Jewel. Ian had been teasing, but he was right. Grant was sexy. Very sexy. I wondered how many other people thought so as well. If others felt as I did, it would be easy to want to pass him through even if they hadn't checked as deeply as they should have.

Lucas nodded and looked over at Xavier. "He's the only one who has the power to dig into people's minds. He hadn't had a chance to dig into Jack's. He was also going to check Bernice. He was there when I talked to her."

I shuddered at the thought of someone like Damien possessing or influencing Bernice. I had a hard time imagining it. Bernice was Bernice and she was solid. If he could get to her, he could get to anyone.

"Bernice, however, has extra spells on her and she's mayor, which adds to her protection," Xavier added looking at me, noticing the shudder.

"So, Damien couldn't have gotten to her and Grant couldn't have released something from her?" I repeated.

"Not likely. Of course, it's highly unlikely that anyone could actually hide Ian, either," Xavier said quietly. "I don't like this."

"We need to recall Randi and Jeremy," Lucas said with a sigh. Randi Arthur was an observer, supposedly impartial, from the U Council, which was the council that governed magic and magical enclaves like Jewel. She made decisions when the people in the enclave might not be able to. She also made sure that any rulings that were enforced by the Council Enforcer, in this case, Jeremy Lirai, were done legally. This was, I'd been told by Ian, because enforcers were taught magic that the rest of us weren't supposed to use. Such spells could be damaging to an enforcer's moral sense.

We'd also had a conclave of people from the U Council here for a few days after Lucas and I had supposedly banished Damien. The dragon-flies had flitted around spitting clover at everyone and hanging close to me, making sure no one bothered me too much. A few of the people from the council who were studying what had happened had found that particularly interesting, but anyone who spent too much time with me or asked too many personal questions tended to lose interest quickly. Not because of anything I had done, but, I suspected, because of the magic of the dragon-flies.

The little creatures were oddly possessive of me, at least around the U Council. They didn't seem particularly bothered by residents of the island.

I hadn't even learned the names of most of the people, but Randi, Jeremy, and Lucas had been the first to arrive and had helped us get rid of Damien. The U Council took our testimonies, matched it to theirs, and eagerly left the island. Probably anxious to get home, or at least wanting to get off an island that had seen more than its fair share of ill-luck and negative magic in the last year.

Xavier was already on the phone. From what I understood, Randi wasn't far from the island. I didn't know if Jeremy had been posted elsewhere, or if he, too, had stayed close. I did know that Randi was one of the people vetting any island visitors.

My scalp tingled. I'd never felt that before. I raised an arm to brush away the tingle.

Lucas frowned.

My arms tingled. Lucas had half-closed his eyes. I suspected he was doing magic, so I calmed myself.

"I get a sense there's a spirit trying to get your attention," Lucas said. "It's not very powerful and I could hardly get a fix on it. It might not be your magic that's taking a hit. It could be that there's something going on with the island and the spirits are struggling."

"Spirits can't be used for power, can they?" I asked.

"Anything can be used for power," Lucas said.

Xavier nodded, though he was clearly on the phone to someone else. He finished the call and dropped his phone back into his pocket.

"Win Bettendorf is nearly here," Xavier said. "She's the Innkeeper that's going to teach Ian. Randi is going to have her call me."

Just then Xavier's phone rang. They certainly didn't waste time. Of course, given what I had learned of the importance of the Innkeeper, I wasn't all that surprised.

Xavier nodded and said little, mostly listening. Then he smiled a bit.

"Win says she can feel Ian. He's on a small boat just off the island. Alone. Someone is trying to get a storm brewing, probably to try and drown him," Xavier said, before he turned to hurry over to the golf cart, which he made go faster than I'd have thought possible for such a small engine.

I rubbed my arms, glancing up at clouds that had suddenly sprung up in the air, heavy dark things that would bring a lot of rain and heavy waves. The lapping of the lake was no longer a splash, but a crash. I couldn't think of anything but Ian out there in a small boat, perhaps even unconscious.

Chapter Six

I glanced at Lucas and he sighed.

"I guess I'll head to the library. It's unfortunate that each enclave has only one place to stay." He looked sadder about the fact that he had no place to go than the fact that Ian was out there on the water, perhaps dying.

I decided that I'd go see Kara down at the dock. It wasn't as if I could do anything for Ian. I don't boat, and while I swim, I don't swim in Lake Michigan in spring when the wind was coming up.

This time the gust hit me just so and the chill went right through me. I hoped that Xavier or whoever he called was able to get to Ian quickly. I wondered who had the magic to create and hold a boat for even a short time. Or maybe the ferry was close enough that Win could do something.

Bernice was good with water. I hoped she knew what was going on and could help.

I felt useless. It seemed to be a typical feeling for me on the island.

In fact, I hadn't felt so useless since I'd been unemployed. I mean, every time something happened on the island, I felt as if I didn't know enough to be helpful. In the last couple of crisis moments, though, people had counted on me, and I'd found a way. This time, I wasn't even being asked. My spirit magic wasn't likely to be of any assistance in finding and saving Ian.

I hated that the one time he needed me, I couldn't help. I'd just left him at the B&B to think. Now, not only was my coworker missing, so was one of my best friends. I kicked at some small stones as I passed by David's clothing store, which was the first building before you got to the little dock.

Jewel's dock was a just long wooden jetty so that the ferry could pull up and let people off. It had a small gravel four car parking lot although no one on the island had a car. A building stood off to one side, so small that it would hardly hold more than one person. For the first time in all the months I'd been on the island, I noticed the door was open.

I headed over there, kicking at pebbles as I went. I hated the way the waves were crashing higher on the shore. I kept thinking of Ian in a boat bobbing around out there.

I'd never been in the little building near the dock. It had always looked abandoned. Maybe it was supposed to. Part of arriving on the island for the first time was finding your way to the B&B. I had heard there were people who managed to get here, but couldn't actually find the place.

Inside, the building was in better condition, which shouldn't have surprised me. There was room for Kara's scooter which sat in a corner. She was in a comfortable looking chair. Another chair, a blue overstuff recliner, waited for me. Wide windows, which I had never noticed from the outside, let us look out over the lake.

"I've never been inside before," Kara said, smiling at

me. "This is new. I might come here now and again when it's a too cold for me to be out on the beach, but I want to watch the waves."

"I haven't been in here, either," I said. "It looks smaller on the outside."

That made Kara laugh, though I missed what I'd said that was funny. When I asked, she waved me off. "I haven't seen anyone come up to the dock."

"I heard that Ian was in a small boat out on the lake. I think Xavier has a fix on where he is and they're going out to get him. The Innkeeper who was coming to teach him more about his powers is on the ferry." I settled into the chair, noticing that, like all chairs on Jewel, it fit me nicely.

"I don't understand who could have that much power. Damien is dead. The dead don't have magic, not that he really had any when he was alive," Kara said. "I heard that they got rid of the people working with Damien, so how did someone get enough power to overcome an Innkeeper while he was in the Inn?"

I shook my head. I had no idea.

"It does make me wonder how Damien found the books that taught him to do the things he did. Looking back, it seems convenient that he found the information he needed," I said.

Kara nodded, thoughtfully. "There are plenty of books on forbidden magics. I suspect that because he wasn't really supposed to be here, he would have been drawn to things that mages aren't supposed to do. There would have been less pressure on him to avoid those things."

I frowned. I hadn't felt any particular pressure to not do certain things.

Kara smiled and responded as if she'd read my mind, a common occurrence on the island. "Oh, I have. I'm a rebel, though. I would love to bring my brother over here even though he's human. I mean, he can visit, but I want him to live here, to understand magic. There are spells I could do to get him here, or force him to hold my hand as I got off the ferry. Whenever I start thinking seriously about it, I get a sense of pressure, like something's holding me back."

Interesting. I had no idea.

"And you said that Damien wouldn't have felt that?" I asked.

"He had no magic, so perhaps not. Or maybe not as strongly. Or else he didn't care," Kara said. "Do you ever notice that when you go to the library there are certain aisles you never want to walk down?"

I cocked my head, thinking about it. There was one right behind Lauren's desk at the library that I always avoided looking at. It seemed darker than the others. I had always figured it was the angle and the light, but maybe Kara was onto something.

"Yeah, actually."

"I made myself go down that one. The one right behind the librarian. I had to make myself pause and look at the books. Even the fonts on the spines were harder to read, but I made myself do it. And I learned a lot of things I'm probably not supposed to know. Just reading them felt icky, like looking at a photo of a particularly injured person or something. I had to force myself to stop thinking about it."

"So anyone on the island could learn those things. They just have to want to badly enough and not care about the consequences," I said quietly.

Kara nodded. "Lauren could do it. She's always there. Doesn't seem to mind the icky places right behind her."

"She's a librarian, though," I said. "Maybe the library

protects her because it's her job. It protected her when people tried to attack her there."

"True. And she'd need to be able to go down that aisle if people asked for information from one of the books." Kara shook her head. "She's a better person than I am if she can resist the impulse to check all that stuff out."

Thinking about Lauren's special bond with the library, I wondered about the U-Council experts. Lucas had to know certain things. He admitted it. Grant Arwen would probably need to know certain things as well. In both cases, not all of them would be good things, but rather, ways to tempt a mage into doing something less than savory.

Had Grant somehow managed to pass the tests done by Randi because he knew how to avoid scrutiny? And of course that charm, the sex appeal that radiated from him could have been a spell. Even I had fallen under it. Maybe his goal had always been to undermine my magic.

Chapter Seven

Watching the waves on the lake can be soothing. I'd done it often enough in between projects at my office. It changed daily from dark blue-green waters to inky black. Sometimes the waves came in small swells splashing playfully against the rocks. At other times they rode higher, crashing against the shore, anger in their movements and sounds.

Today, nothing soothed. The crashing reminded me that Xavier was out trying to rescue Ian, stuck in a small boat. I hoped that whoever was helping could lead them to Ian. I wanted to be there, not just watching and waiting, but no one had asked me to go. I didn't know enough about where Ian might be to even try to follow, and believe me, I'd considered it.

Kara was silent in her chair, watching the waves. I wondered if it was meditative for her, but didn't ask. I didn't want to intrude if she wasn't feeling talkative. She stayed up so late working, and when I saw her around on the beach during the daylight hours, it always seemed as if she were meditating, avoiding sleep for some reason.

The fog began to roll in, tendrils reaching up toward

the island, grabbing on and pushing themselves higher and thicker in the air.

"Ferry's almost here," Kara said in her quiet voice. She didn't move, though.

I stood, hoping to go meet the new Innkeeper. Besides, I was restless, not doing enough. Watching the waves only made me more aware of what we were up against trying to find Ian. I had no idea where and how Xavier was searching, nor how far the boat might be washed from where it had been when Win felt Ian out there.

Ian was alone. If he was awake, he'd probably be terrified. I knew I would be. It'd be especially bad if something had cut him off from his magic. That's the only way they could have gotten him off the island. Cut the link, at least briefly. Of course, if Ian were unconscious, it wouldn't matter as much. He couldn't use magic if he wasn't aware.

Outside, I heard the ferry's horn, mournful in the fog. I had noticed the fog the first day. Everyone else on the boat had gone inside, away from the moist clouds. I wondered if they were ever curious about why they hit such thick fog in the middle of the lake on an otherwise beautiful day. Magic probably kept ordinary people from wondering.

I saw the white and red ferry pull up to the dock. The engines were loud against the quiet of the island. I was once again reminded of how peaceful Jewel was, and how thankful I was for that peacefulness. Too bad we couldn't seem to get rid of the problems that Damien had unleashed.

An elderly woman walked slowly down the ramp, using a rollator. She had a carry-on bag in the cart in front of her and with one hand she pulled at a larger suitcase making her progress very slow.

I hurried up the ramp to help her with the bag.

"Thank you, dear," she said. "I'm Win."

"I'm Holly Baxter. I'm Jewel's accountant…and Ian's friend."

"The last I knew—your energy is mixed up with his. I can smell it," Win smiled.

I kind of blanched at the idea of her smelling me. And, while her smile was friendly, there was something not quite human about her eyes. Perhaps their sharpness was at odds with the aging of the rest of her body.

Win laughed a bit. "It's my magical ability. I smell magic and auras. It's nothing personal, nor am I suggesting you stink. You and Ian are linked by friendship. You've been through a lot together."

"We have," I said. "I'm so worried about him."

"Your sheriff has found him and is guiding the boat back in," Win said.

"I didn't even know we had another boat on the island. I expected they'd go out from here. When they didn't… I figured they were working from the shore…" I trailed off. I'd imagined Xavier standing on a rock overlooking the far side of the lake, lasso whipping around his head, ready to send it off to pull Ian's little boat in, which, of course, looked like a rowboat in my imagination.

"Someone has the magic to create one," Win said. "You're new so, of course, haven't had time to find out all the tricks of the enclaves. I'm happy to teach what I know when I'm not with Ian."

I decided I liked Win. Before the ramp to the ferry went up, two other people hurried down. I recognized the very tall, dark, and handsome Jeremy Lirai. Beside him, Randi Arthur was nearly invisible, though on her own, she was a lovely woman.

"Holly," Randi greeted me when they caught up to me and Win.

"Randi," I said.

"I see you finally found your way off," Win said quietly, smiling.

"We were looking for you," Randi said. "I thought you'd need help."

"I figured someone would come," Win replied easily. "And I was right."

Randi shook her head, but said nothing. Jeremy just looked beyond us, scanning the island.

"I don't like the feel here. Something is off. Not like last time. Last time mages did it. This time it's something deeper," he said quietly.

Randi closed her eyes and stood still. Win waited.

"I can feel it, barely." Randi glanced at Win.

"There's no Innkeeper right now," Win said. "I feel that. He's okay, but off the island, on a boat being guided back in."

"But what allowed the Innkeeper to be taken?" Jeremy asked. "I feel that. Something or someone has put a damper on the island itself."

"This morning," I said, "I had an incident. I felt Sharon's presence, but I couldn't see her. Didn't even really know she was there. It was like my magic was gone. Just for an instant. Lucas and I thought that I had wavered in my ability to accept those parts of myself that my magic comes from."

Win didn't ask for clarification on who Sharon was. Perhaps she'd read up on our recent escapades on the island. Jeremy and Randi, of course, would have heard about what she'd done when they'd been here such a short time ago.

Jeremy frowned. "Was there a reason you would have lost that ability for a short time?"

I shrugged a bit, uncomfortable beneath his stare. In many ways, Jeremy was more handsome than Grant

Arwen, but Jeremy was also more distant, less interested, perhaps. I didn't feel a need to be anything other than what I was with him.

"I think so," I said softly.

Randi put a hand on my arm. "We won't question further. If we do, it will be with only one of us, whoever you're most comfortable with. We'll dig in your memories, too, if that helps, so you don't have to talk about it. For now, it's something we can file away as a possible clue."

Jeremy kept his lips pressed tightly together, assessing me, but he gave a nod to Randi.

Win had kept on walking, pushing her rollator ahead. I hurried to catch up. Randi and Jeremy had only small cases with them, of the sort that Win had tucked in her basket. She intended to stay awhile. The other two, just for a few days. Or perhaps, being younger, they had fewer needs.

The wind whipped around us. I hoped Xavier had gotten Ian to the shore and was bringing him back to the Inn.

Win paused at the front of the Victorian. The Japanese maple was once again budding out. The paint colors were still faded. The cats weren't around.

When Win laid a hand on the gate, I watched as the colors brightened, like the face of loved one who was finally getting to see someone they thought lost. Win gave a single nod. The orange cat came around the side of the building and watched us, but didn't come close. I didn't see the other two.

"The B&B will let us in," Win said. "And we're in no danger from it. It can feel Ian now, too. The link was blocked, but through me, it found him and disengaged the block. Does the island feel different now?"

Win didn't look at Jeremy, but I knew she was asking him. He'd been the one to feel the wrongness.

"It's still there. Weaker, but there. You snapped a link, perhaps, but didn't get the core of the spell," Jeremy said. He didn't step onto the B&B's grounds, though Randi did. Instead, he stood there looking at the place. Then he pulled out a cell phone and made a call.

I heard Jeremy speak the words "Code Red," the sound brushing by me in the breeze, making me shiver, or maybe it was the wind. I couldn't be certain. But every book, every movie, every TV show I'd watched that had the term "Code Red" had it meaning that something had gone very, very wrong and we needed immediate help.

My body felt weak from the recent battle with Damien. I also still felt a bit vulnerable from my encounter with Grant Arwen. As if something had been ripped from me, leaving me raw and unsure of myself. Unfortunately, I had no idea exactly what that might be.

Whatever Code Red meant, I didn't feel up to dealing with it. I thought longingly of the ferry that was already on its way to Wisconsin. I wished I were on it.

Chapter Eight

I stayed outside the fence of the B&B while Win went inside. Jeremy and Randi seemed torn. Randi finally set down her bag just inside the fence. Jeremy did the same and the two headed back down the street the way we had come. I followed, though no one asked me. I figured that they hadn't told me not to come, so I would, until and unless someone got annoyed with me tagging along.

Randi turned to me, slowing. Jeremy kept up the quick pace and was soon ahead of us. While the wind still blew hard enough to whip her chin-length hair around her face, the dark clouds were beginning to scatter. As if they'd been called to create weather that would capsize Ian's boat and drown him just off the island.

"I don't have Jeremy's ability to sense the island, just people," Randi said. She spoke quietly, looking around as if that was news. People went about their business in the grocery store. I waved at Sandra, my neighbor, as she came out. She nodded at me, frowning when she saw Randi.

Randi waited until she was out of ear shot. "I don't like

that Ian was able to be smuggled off the island and his link to the B&B interrupted, even for a short time. I don't like that your magic was tested as well. I feel as if someone is testing the limits of the strongest magic users on the island."

"Jack is missing, though," I said. "I know Jack has magic, but is he that strong?"

Randi shook her head. "Had Grant Arwen met with Jack before he disappeared?"

"He went in and set up a time to meet with Jack," I said.

"It's possible that there was some link to Jack, a sort of time bomb set to go off once Grant arrived. We do have certain expected routines in place once an enclave has had problems. Someone who was familiar with those—and this group would have been, considering Marielle was an officer in Hidden Rock."

Marielle had been one of the people who had worked alongside a spirit magician who was attempting to help Damien possess me so he could get back on the island. I had no doubt my death would have been part of that. She'd been taken away to Far Haven, the magical prison island.

The idea made sense. Jack, or the mage who influenced him, could have been the one to create a spell to get me so interested in Grant Arwen that I'd start questioning myself. Most people tended to be sensitive about their looks. As heavy as I was, it would be a logical leap that I'd second guess myself if I were overly attracted to a particular man. I mean, our culture told me to be sensitive a million times a day. No one is completely immune.

"I think Grant Arwen was working over in the library," I said. "He had other people to examine. Could Damien be possessing Jack somehow? I know he doesn't have spirit magic, but it seems like it's a stretch for this to be someone just influencing him."

"Lucas has been fairly certain Damien is gone. And you didn't see Damien in the office. You saw Sharon, when you finally saw someone," Randi said.

I nodded. I was pretty sure it had been Sharon, but I couldn't be absolutely certain. I hadn't been at my best. I'd been doubting myself. And maybe someone had put in that sliver of doubt and then tried to utilize my magic.

"How does it work, really," I asked Randi, seeing she seemed to feel rather talkative, "when we doubt ourselves and lose magic? Can it happen just that fast or is it the sort of thing that usually creeps up on people?"

"Normally it's something that creeps up on people," Randi said. "Which is why I have my suspicions about your sudden inability to use your magic. It's not impossible, in the right circumstances, to have personal acceptance implode, so to speak, but by the time we get magic and have been here, it's unlikely. Everything in our enclaves is designed to make us think about and accept all of ourselves, or as much as it can be."

She was right. Things appeared when people needed them. I had learned from Kara, for instance, that when she wanted to go up the stairs to Derry's, an elevator appeared for her rather than her having to try and figure out the stairs. The elevator worked much like their stairwell. The minute she rolled inside, she was on the upper level, wherever that was, exactly.

Derry's location was one of the many riddles of the island. I mean everyone knew how to get there, but where the "there" was, was a mystery.

It was hard to be ashamed of being different on the

island. There was an awareness that all of us had things we were ashamed of and we working on accepting ourselves. In those areas where we couldn't just fit in quietly, the island made sure accessibility was easy for everyone.

Jeremy reached the police station, the low building all brown wood and glass. Beyond and across the narrow street was the library building, a two story thing that might have been a small office complex anywhere but on the island.

The station was Jeremy's goal, but as I started to follow, Randi put a hand on my arm. "Let's go to the library," she said.

I followed her, glancing back at the station a few times. I really wanted to know if Rose had an update from Xavier about Ian. Instead, I followed Randi to see what she wanted in the library.

We were barely inside, walking across the plush burgundy carpet, when Lauren noticed us, giving me a wave, frowning a little at Randi. It wasn't a frown of dislike, but rather a perplexed look. Randi paused by the desk.

"Ian went missing," she said quietly. Even more quietly than she'd spoken to me.

"And Jack," I added.

Lauren's eyes had gotten big when Randi told her about Ian. I remembered when Jack wasn't quite Jack and had told me that Lauren had a crush on Ian. The two couldn't be less alike. Ian was all gossip and outgoing, with a fashion sense that ran to black jeans and plaid vests. Lauren was quieter with an eye for fashion that I envied. Tailored suits and dresses, along with a selection of scarves larger than my entire wardrobe, or so it seemed. She always had one tied around her neck, brightening up whatever outfit she had on.

It was only recently that I learned that Lauren hadn't been raised as a girl like I was. The scarves, I suspected, were a way to hide an Adam's apple that was larger than that of most women. Had Jack not mentioned it back when he'd gossiped about Lauren's crush, I'd never have noticed and just thought she had thing for scarves.

"Is Grant around?" Randi asked.

Lauren nodded. "He's in the small conference room in the far corner." Lauren's voice was a bit lower than I expected, but it made her sound like a sexy, sultry star in an old movie.

I could tell she wanted to ask more about Ian, but Randi was already leaving. I paused to let her know that Win had told me that Xavier was pulling Ian back onto the island. Lauren's shoulders relaxed almost imperceptibly.

"Thank heavens," she whispered. Then she nodded at me to go after Randi.

I needed to hurry. I could imagine Randi getting to the office Grant was using and closing the door in my face.

Hurrying along a path I didn't normally take, I followed the U council observer. I knew that the big room off to the side of the main library had meeting rooms, but I'd only ever been over there once, when Lauren had been too injured to actually open the library. The rooms were the usual conference type rooms with dividers that could be re-arranged to create a room sized for the group. Today, all dividers were in place, so that the library had plenty of reasonably sized offices with a hallway down the middle.

The burgundy carpet continued, but instead of books, the rooms smelled of cleaning supplies. The walls were a neutral cream and the partition sections were outlined in white with the white tracks on the floor barely visible.

The doors were all closed, but Randi walked confidently to the end one and knocked.

"Come in!" Grant called. I felt my body tingle at the sound of his voice. It made my blood sing. I'd never felt like that, even with my ex-husband.

Randi glanced at me and frowned slightly. Then she nodded to herself and went in.

The room was longer than it was wide. Grant sat at a computer on a small table towards the back, the window behind him, highlighting his dark hair. He looked surprised to see Randi.

My arms tingled as one of them did magic. Randi had stilled, so I suspected it was her. I didn't like the way Grant's eyes narrowed as he intuited what she was doing.

"You've already checked me once," he snapped.

Randi said nothing. The tingling along my arms got stronger.

Grant closed his eyes. I felt more magic in the air. The tingling in my arms intensified. No one had managed to show me a spell that would keep me from feeling magic when others did it. Normally, it was a minor thing. Today, it was painful.

Pain meant heavy magic. I put up a protection spell, a light one, hoping that the other two wouldn't notice. I had no idea what they were doing, magically. The tingling continued. Protection spells didn't protect me from the pain of someone else doing magic, unfortunately.

Randi waved a hand. "How did you get past me?" she finally asked.

"I didn't," Grant said. "Grant did."

As if he wasn't actually Grant. Then the person that I thought had been Grant smiled. "I've been waiting for someone with his talents for some time. Hidden inside Jack all this time…"

"How long?" I demanded, stepping forward,

wondering if Jack hadn't been himself ever or if this was another trick like when Damien had influenced him. Maybe it was possible to leave a kernel of something inside another person.

"Since a week after Jack arrived on the island. How do you think it was so easy to hide inside him? He was always a weak human, but without me there they wouldn't have been able to influence him to such an extent. I've had such hope for so long… riding under the radar… It was good to get out. To see the way the world has changed…finally." Grant, or whoever it was, shook his head.

The annoying thing was, he was still really attractive, really handsome.

Something rolled off my protection spell. I felt the magic hit, strong stuff, but he hadn't expected a protection spell. I could hold them for a very long time now.

Randi stumbled back, though, and held her head. She shook it several times and then glared at him. "You should know that all of us who represent the enclaves get spelled to protect us against things like you."

"As did Grant." Again that smile, an evil smile. Not the nice one from the office, from before I went to get Jack. Maybe Grant was really a decent guy inside all that.

"Who are you?" I asked. Magic tingled along my arms.

Randi had her eyes closed and did something, some magic.

"I am the first of the mages on Jewel. Do you know how enclaves are made? You don't, I suppose. No one talks about it. They take a person with an affinity to the land in the area, or the lake, in this case, and sacrifice them. Only blood will do. And a heart. It is my heart that links the magic to the enclave." Again that smile.

"Don't believe it," Randi said quietly. "The heart came

from a willing mage, usually an old mage who was dying anyway. Moments before their death, they'd take the heart and do the spells that would create a new enclave. It's given generously."

"Mine wasn't!" he snapped.

"I suspect," Randi said, "That if we look at the history of Jewel, we'll find a number of small incidents where people played around with harmful magic, letting it seep into the grounds. Magic has a sentience but it doesn't understand. Sometimes spirits that hang around can get bored. They enjoy making trouble. The more trouble, the more harmful magic, the darker the enclave can get. Except there's a purity to the natural magic so that it can't ever be completely overcome. This one is a product of the small insults, coloring his memories of his world and the enclave."

Grant, which I would call this man for lack of a better name, just smirked. "Believe what you want."

My arms barely tingled when he pushed his hand out, sending a pulse of energy at us. It pushed me so hard that I stumbled backwards and into the wall. Randi was right beside me. She pushed out with a hand and forced the energy back towards Grant.

"Go," she whispered to me.

My arms tingled as I left the room. I heard a small sound and then Randi was next to me.

"If he's the heart of the island, shouldn't he be more powerful?" I asked.

"He's a spirit, inhabiting Grant's body. Probably managed to hop over while Grant was concentrating on scheduling with Jack. He's powerful because he's the link between humanity and the magic so he has some magic that spirits normally don't. I expect he had Jack's magic as well, which was probably more considerable than most of us thought."

Randi hurried me down the hall, back to the library, though no one followed us. She closed her eyes. Once again, she did magic but this was normal magic, making my arms tingle and itch, not hurt.

Then she did something else that was more powerful. Lauren hurried over to us, probably feeling something from Randi while she worked.

"I've sealed him in the building," Randi said. "Keep the door locked and don't let anyone through."

Lauren frowned and nodded. "What's happened?"

"Grant has been taken over by a spirit. An old one linked to creation of the island," Randi said. She pulled out her phone and made a call.

Lauren looked up towards the ceiling, thinking. "We have books on the enclave's creation. They'll include names and stories about the people involved, at least the ones they thought would be important."

She walked over to her desk to search where the books were, and probably to start reading. I felt at a loss. I wasn't any help. My stomach was still in knots thinking about Ian. Guilt hit me then, that I hadn't hardly thought about Jack at all while worrying about Ian. Now that I realized that, I wanted to know where he was, if he was okay or if that spirit had done something to him.

It made me sad to think that all the time he'd been on the island, no one had ever really known Jack. He was a quiet man but perhaps his quiet ways had been influenced by the spirit that was inside him, waiting for a mage with the right powers to come along that it could influence.

"Go have a seat," Randi said. "Win is on her way, as is Jeremy. Your Chief of Police has dropped Ian off at the clinic. He's not hurt, but someone put a powerful spell on him to knock him out."

"I could go over to the clinic," I said.

Randi shook her head. "You have too much spirit magic and something may be working on getting to you. I want you where we can observe what happens."

My heart sank. I was around not because I could be helpful, but because Randi didn't think I could be trusted.

Chapter Nine

Jeremy was at the library in no time, practically flying through the doors. He didn't greet anyone, just walked in, past the tables, to the door where Randi waited. I felt a slight tingling on my arms when he did magic, probably to check Randi's magic or add to it. Then he nodded, glanced around, his hazel eyes falling on me.

He walked over to the table. My arms tingled again, though he made no move as if doing magic. Even Bernice sometimes stiffens slightly.

"You're clear, so far," he said. "But stay around. I've called in more enforcers, all of them tough. One of them will always be with you."

Win came in with her rollator and spotted us. She nodded her gray head in acknowledgement.

"I felt it when you contained him," she said. "The island feels better. Not perfect. Far from it. The longer I stayed in the B&B, the more I felt the rot. No wonder Ian hasn't ever come up to his full powers. He probably didn't want to go too deep in order to avoid the sensation. He wouldn't have known, of course, because it was always there."

"We might need to tear down the enclave and start again," Jeremy said. He looked Win up and down.

Win shook her head. "I'm not ready to go. And I certainly don't want to be linked to an enclave that's not mine for all eternity. Gads. You think this one was bad. I'd be worse. No."

Jeremy smiled a bit. "It was a thought. You'd be a good heart no matter what you say."

Win waved a hand at him. Then she moved her rollator over and settled in a chair near mine. She looked at me for a moment before speaking.

"You're clear. I can feel that. I'm sure Jeremy put you through a spell or something. It's more thorough than my sense. However, I do get a sense that the island wants you. Damien wanted you and implanted that idea in the island. There are others that make up the island's history and energy that loved you which makes the pull stronger," Win said looking at me. "They'll want Jeremy and Randi for their power and their access to other enclaves. You, they want for yourself. You have such strong spirit magic, that allows them avenues to get to you that aren't available with Jeremy and Randi and whoever he's called in."

Great. Once again I was a target and I didn't understand why exactly.

"Should I leave the island? Will that let them work better?" I asked Win. I didn't want to leave, even for a short time, but if it would allow the others find whatever or whoever was behind this, then I'd do it. Hopefully not for long. I'd come to love Jewel.

At Christmas, I'd gone to my oldest sister's and I'd missed Ian and my friends on the island. I'd even missed Bernice. Ian and I texted and messaged back and forth, but that wasn't Bernice's thing. I loved being with my sisters and their children, but it wasn't the same as being on Jewel. And I'd remembered how hard it could be to find a chair that fit me.

"They haven't asked and I don't see the advantage. They got to Alexander Milton off island. And he was far more prepared for a fight than you are," Win said.

Her words sort of hurt. I'd worked hard to be prepared against any attack. Bernice had armed me well to be sure I couldn't be used.

"Don't take it personally," Win said. "I'm not as well armed as Alexander. Even Jeremy isn't and he's the best enforcer the Council has. He's probably a bit more on edge when he travels because the guards at Far Haven have fewer enemies than enforcers do."

She cocked her head and shook it a little. As she did so, I heard the front door of the library open and Bernice and Xavier came in. Lucas trailed them, looking worried.

"Lucas. Yes. Now, he's one that might be in more danger than you are," Win said. "He doesn't have your power, but he's trained."

"How do you know all this?" I asked.

"I have a certain amount of telepathy," Win said. "My job as the Innkeeper expands it. While I'm not very powerful outside of an enclave, in one, I am. Though here, not nearly so much as at my own place. Still, all enclaves are linked. I should be able to send Ian messages once we set up a link. I can with the others. It's one reason I was sent here in addition to adding to his training. Everyone thought it was his fault that he was slow to learn. Clearly, it wasn't."

I wasn't sure how to feel about sitting with someone with telepathy. So far as I knew Ian didn't have it. He loved talking to people and he loved finding out secrets. He'd intimated that part of his shameful issues revolved around being nosey, though I wasn't quite sure how much that was it. Even so, if he could read minds, he'd have been over the moon. I doubt he'd have ever made jokes about being nosey. He'd just know things.

I was well aware that no two people had exactly the same type of magic, though, so Ian's magic was no doubt quite different from Win's.

Lucas plopped down across from us. Bernice marched over to nod at all of us, her expression giving nothing away.

"I heard Ian was found and he's okay," I said.

"He is. Dr. Mulrooney is with him. He's lucky Win was able to get a fix on him. It seems we have more issues with the island than we expected," Bernice said. Although she stared at me as if she felt it was my fault, I knew that she was just speaking her mind and didn't mean that I should have known anything.

Bernice was tough, but I'd learned that she was fair. She was the sort of woman who worked for respect and rarely let her feelings get in the way of what she saw as her job. Before, her job had been teaching people new to the enclave how to use their magic. Now, she was the acting mayor. Given the situations she'd managed to guide the island through in the last few months, I figured she ought to be able to win any mayoral contest.

Lauren returned with a pile of books. Bernice went over and grabbed a couple, putting one in front of me and one in front of Lucas.

"Lauren is fast but more eyes are faster," Bernice said. "I want you to find out anything you can about the history of the island, particularly about the founders."

I opened the old leather bound volume, unsurprised when dust floated up from it. The pages were thick, yellowed vellum and I felt rather like I was in a movie, reading an old book. I half expected to feel a shock of magic and receive a curse.

"The island would negate any curses," Win said in a low voice. Then she gave me a conspiratorial grin. "I was thinking the same thing. I'm glad Bernice just assumes my eyesight isn't what it used to be. That's one thing that still works, though. Too bad. There are other things I'd rather have work better."

I smiled back at her. Win was definitely enchanting me —and not in the way Grant Arwen had done, with his blue eyes and sexy smile and ever so slight once over. She made me feel confident and not silly about the sometimes ridiculous thoughts and leaps I made when finding something out about Jewel.

Lucas sneezed over his book.

Lauren looked up. "I have masks," she said. "I don't want people sneezing on the books. The magic helps preserve them, but nothing is fool-proof and dampness is the bane of a book's existence."

Lucas got up and grabbed a couple. He gave one to me and took one for himself. Win just smiled and nodded at him.

Bernice and Xavier were over with Jeremy and Randi near the door Randi had spelled. Randi talked with her hands more than the others. Xavier looked concerned. Bernice gave away almost nothing. She rarely did. Jeremy was nearly as difficult to read, but he moved a bit more, lacking Bernice's ability to stand completely still, with perfect posture, for long periods of time.

His eyes roamed the room like a cop looking for a villain. He also shifted his weight more. Now and then, the corner of his eye twitched slightly. I didn't know him well enough to know what those things meant, but at least he had cues, if I learned to read them. It certainly wouldn't be difficult to watch him long enough to learn, though no doubt he'd be gone in a few weeks, once again.

I mean, he was lovely to look at, but the fact that he was here meant there were problems on Jewel. I'd rather the island be the nice safe place it felt like it should be rather than an enclave with a horror at its heart.

"There's no horror," Win said. "Just an angry spirit. Literally. It's picked up on every negative thing in the enclave, which is too bad. It's why the people who are willing to be used to start an enclave are interviewed so carefully. It's easy to pick up the negativity of so many people, particularly when you have nothing but the energies of emotions to hold you somewhere, and a link that won't let you go."

"I almost think we'd learn more just interviewing you," I said quietly.

Lucas chuckled. "She's only saying what most of the people in the enclave council know already. It might be new to you and most of the civilians on the island, but not to people like Jeremy and Randi. If they think there's an issue, there's definitely an issue and we need to find out where it comes from and who the spirit is. I'll probably have to see about banishing as much of the negativity as I can, but I'll need a name and probably some further information on him. And any particularly powerful negative influences."

"Like Damien," I said.

"He was just the last. Probably the strongest because he was the most recent and the heart spirit had so much to work with, but he won't be the catalyst," Lucas said.

"I don't understand. It seemed like the island was helping me," I said.

"We are all the sum of many parts," Win said. "It's

why being the Innkeeper takes so long and slows down our aging. We have much to learn. We need the time to learn it and then work with it to keep an enclave going. I believe the innkeeper before Ian was killed. Grace was a lovely woman. We were contemporaries, if you can believe it. She died rather suddenly. Now, I suspect she had help."

Lucas pulled out his phone and made a few notes, probably to get Grace's name and how she died.

Win shook herself as if waking from a dream. "The important part is that you wanted to know how the island could like you, want to protect you, and also destroy you. The island is the magic, but it's also the people. The love came from a relative's spirit who was feeding Damien's magic. Those conflicting feelings spread to the magic. However, the heart has a destructive part in the original founder, who is frustrated. I have a feeling we'll need someone new to become part of the island. It's hard to get rid of the rot once it starts."

"How would that work?" I asked.

"They'll have several enclave enforcers and representatives here, along with Win and Ian, to hold the island as it is," Lucas said. "Then I'll have to cut the cord to the old heart spirit. A new person will have to die and we'll need to use their heart to solidify the magic of the island again. And before you vomit all over the table, the person must be willing. We carefully vet them or we end up in the same position we're in now, or perhaps worse. I'll be able to pull some cords of negativity from the island, but at some point in the not too distant future, there'll need to be a new heart."

"I think you're right," Win said. "If it were my enclave, I would volunteer, but this isn't my home and I can't see myself here for eternity. It has to be someone else."

I didn't know anyone on the island who was that old.

There were many older people here, but no one who seemed close to dying. Of course, I didn't know everyone. I guess Sharon had cancer and had been close to death when she'd made her pact with Damien to live forever.

"Sharon would be another negative influence," I said.

"And I'll banish her, too, if she's not already gone" Lucas said. "I'll no doubt have help. Jeremy has some affinity for spirit magic, but he's not that strong. Spirit isn't always a good thing for an enforcer, though there are a few like me who only seem to have spirit magic. They don't teach. They're not experts, but they have power. Probably even more than you do and you have a considerable amount."

Win gave Lucas a long look but said nothing. I wasn't sure what to make of that. It almost seemed as if she were thinking about what should be said. It made me slightly uncomfortable when people said I had power. I didn't even really understand what that meant. And, of course, I had no idea how to use it.

I'd have liked to have asked what Win thought, but knew if she didn't want to speak, she wouldn't. Instead, I turned another dusty page, and stared at the words, trying to make sense of them. The writing was tiny, the handwriting curling and styled making it difficult to read. Further, I wasn't at all sure I knew what I was looking for.

I pulled out my phone so I could make notes, hoping that I didn't miss anything important. Hoping that my eyes would handle the words that seemed scrunched together like the writer was trying to economize on paper. No doubt they were, and given the size of the book, I couldn't blame them. I flipped ahead a few pages, trying to get a sense of what was in the tome, but even that was slow going.

I caught a name, read more closely. Realized it was the

name we were looking for. Ambrose Marchand, the man who had given his heart to the enclave.

"I found it," I said. "It's..."

Win put a hand on my arm and shook her head. Lucas looked terrified, putting a finger to his mouth.

They'd stopped me before I could make another major mistake.

I hated the landmines of magic that I didn't understand. Instead, I turned the book towards Lucas so he could see the name, read it, and prepare to do what he had to.

Chapter Ten

Lucas nodded at the name and turned the book back to me. He glanced around at the others and made a note on his phone.

Win looked over my shoulder, curious. Then, she too nodded. I heard the group at the door whispering, but I couldn't quite make out the words. Even as Lucas turned, Jeremy looked up. He looked at all of us, and, for just an instant, held my eyes.

Like Grant, he was dark-haired, but his eyes were hazel. I had always thought Jeremy would make the perfect love interest in a thriller movie, the way he looked and moved. Grant had charisma and he knew how to use it. Jeremy didn't seem to notice that he was sexy, or if he did, he didn't care.

I really needed to meet a man. I was having fantasies all over the place. It happens when you get older and the libido rises. Oddly I hadn't been aware of how much I needed to meet someone until today. Suddenly, I was hormonal all over the place.

I'd dated a man on the island, but the sparks weren't

really there. He had an ex who could make my life difficult, which was not how I wanted to start my life on Jewel. Instead, we'd parted friends and he'd gone back to his ex, which, according to Ian, was something that seemed to happen a lot with this particular couple.

A faint scent of dust brought me back to the book in front of me. The thick pages and the old spines made a creak as my hand rested on it. I was aware, over the whispers, of Lauren turning pages in her book.

I went back to reading about Ambrose Marchand. He'd been a French trapper in his day. At some point he'd discovered his magic. There wasn't an enclave around, so he'd headed south, something drawing him. If asked by ordinary folks, he would have said warmer weather.

The nearest enclave had been outside of what is now Toronto. Ambrose had, according to the records, been led there by a beaver. I had expected a giant silvery elk, but no, it was a beaver. A pretty ordinary one that just wouldn't get caught and kept moving southeast. Something inside Ambrose compelled him to pursue the creature.

Ambrose had taken to magic. He'd had mostly water magic, with some earth magic. He'd not been a particularly powerful mage. In fact, if he hadn't been listed as founding Jewel Island, I doubted he'd have been remembered. He'd lived up around the Toronto enclave for most of his life, never taking a wife, at least not after he found his magic.

I noted that nothing in the book mentioned what his secret shame was. I wondered what people several hundred years ago were ashamed of. Was it a lack of faith? Had Ambrose been ashamed of not marrying? Or perhaps losing his family? There was some intimation that he'd once been married and hints of a tragedy.

When the enclave started outgrowing its space,

searchers had been sent out to find a new place to anchor another enclave. As he was old and dying, Ambrose had volunteered to go with them. He'd ridden in a cart because he could no longer walk easily. One of the searchers had an inkling that there was a possibility of creating an island in Lake Michigan.

Several of the searchers took out boats to find the exact coordinates where they should found this enclave. One of them felt something described as a resonance near where Jewel was today.

Several mages with earth magic raised an island from the bottom of the lake and there they performed the ceremony that anchored Ambrose's spirit to the enclave.

As I read, I became engrossed in the story, losing track of the sounds of anyone else turning pages or the whispers that swirled around. I didn't notice when Win moved away, though I had a sense that the warm comfort I'd been feeling was gone.

When I looked up, I noticed that both Win and Lucas were over by the door. I was the only one left reading at the table. I frowned, wishing someone had tapped me on the shoulder instead of quietly going on their way. Lauren was still at her desk, as absorbed in her reading as I had been.

I pushed myself up from the chair and walked over. Randi and Jeremy were at the door. My arms tingled from the magic they were performing. Either it was light enough magic that I hadn't felt it halfway across the library or they'd just started.

Bernice and Xavier stood silently. Lucas had his arms on Randi's shoulders, perhaps feeding her energy. If she needed his magic, then it wasn't a small spell at all.

The tingle got stronger. Nausea hit me suddenly. I put a hand over my mouth and looked around for a bathroom. While a moment ago, there had only been a little seating area under the stairs, now a bathroom with an open door beckoned me.

I hurried inside, making it to the toilet before I made a mess. I had no idea what started the nausea.

Win came in while I was resting in there, taking in the shiny white toilet and the wide single stall that almost gave me privacy, or would if I had managed to close the door. The small white tiles were shiny and clean. Even the white sinks hanging on the wall looked newly set into the long blue counter. The walls were painted the same blue, a dark color that reminded me of the lake in winter. A painting of a large black stallion hung on the wall I could see reflected in the big mirror.

Oddly, despite what I'd just done, the room didn't stink. It was quiet, considering that the door was open to the main library. My arms didn't even tingle, though deep down I knew the magic was still being done.

"I think that Lucas may have missed a bit of influence in you," Win said, patting my shoulder. "So did I. And I was looking. I doubt he was. But I know how easy it is to get sucked into these things and you were so attracted to Grant Arwen."

"Was that what this was?" I asked. I leaned back, hating to sit on the floor of a public restroom, but I didn't know whether or not I was going to need the toilet again. At least this one was clean. I mean, it had sort of been created just for me to vomit in. Another plus to living on a magical island.

"It was," Win said. She settled on the seat on her rollator where she'd held her carry-on bag. She put a lock on it so it didn't roll out from under her and looked at me.

"You would be a prize. If you were the prize, then it seems like they may have used Jack to influence you. There are a million ways to disguise influence. It's less that you'd been fully influenced, but more that the seeds of it were planted, hoping that someone with power could make them grow and bloom. It's why everyone missed it," Win said, nodding to herself.

I wondered what else she was thinking. It seemed like there was more to her thoughts than just what she'd told me, but my stomach was still threatening to turn inside out and I didn't have enough focus to ask questions.

Win placed a hand on my arm and things began to tingle. Not just my arm, but my whole body.

My stomach calmed and I felt clearer headed. I breathed in.

"Thank you," I said.

"I'm not sure it's done," she said. "If I couldn't feel influence right away, I don't trust that I'll feel when you're completely clean, but that should allow you to rest a bit. If something more comes up, we'll know it was the spell they're doing."

"Why didn't Randi do that for everyone on the island after we cleared Damien out? And why not do it for anyone coming to Jewel?" I asked.

My stomach did a little flip and then a flop. I felt clearer after that, as if another layer of influence had cleared.

"It takes a lot of magic to do such spells. You may have noticed Lucas lending some support to Randi and Jeremy, who were working together. They're attempting to clear out any influence on Grant, but the spells leak, so they're probably getting anyone near the library." Win moved slightly making her rollator creak a bit. It was loud in the quiet bathroom.

"I doubt there's anyone in the enclave council, enforcer or witness, who has enough power to do this spell more than once a day, even with help," Win continued.

I wasn't sure if I were lucky or not.

"I guess I was lucky to be here," I said. "I wonder how many other people might have some influence that needs to be cleared."

Win sighed. "I'm not sure of the last time there was an attempt to overthrow an enclave. Not in recent history. Pine-on-Lakes probably, and they lost the enclave completely, but that was a whole other story."

"Pine-on-Lakes?" I asked. What a difficult name to remember. Thankfully, Jewel was much easier.

"Right?" Win gave me a conspiratorial grin. "It happened before I came into my magic, probably by about a decade and I came into magic early. It wasn't okay for women to be sexual in my day, you know."

I tried to keep a straight face, but then Win gave me a wink and wiggled her hips on her rollator and I lost it.

She nodded. "So I had my shame and acceptance…"

I held up a hand. "I thought we weren't supposed to talk about our shame?"

"I'm an Innkeeper. Just try and use it against me. You'll be using it against my entire enclave," Win laughed. "And besides, it's silly now. And that's probably why I'm one of the more powerful Innkeepers."

I felt something at the base of my neck, a tingle in my arms. Win was looking out the door so I didn't think she was using magic. She turned back to me.

"At any rate, that's how long ago it was. I'm older than I look and I know I look plenty old," she told me, less sassy, more conspiratorial. "Pine-on-Lakes had a mayor subvert the enclave's magic. They did some blood sacrifices outside the enclave, just on the edge, where the magic began. That, is, I suppose, an advantage, or disadvantage, of not being an island, there are exact boundaries that you prob-ably can't feel here on Jewel. They could splash the blood into the enclave and utilize it for their wants. Happened enough to tarnish the enclave."

I heard chanting coming from beyond the door.

"Dear," Win paused, also looking out, "They are really going all in."

She turned back to me. "At any rate, the tarnish got deeper, darker. The U council came in and tried to take down the mayor. The first enforcer was taken down. Not killed, of course. Just wounded and bound. Others came in and surrounded the enclave. When all was said and done, the heart of the enclave wasn't just tarnished and darkened, it was broken. The heart said it couldn't go on, wouldn't even wait for a new heart to be found. The Innkeeper was bereft. I can only imagine how that hurt. We're linked to the heart, you know."

I nodded. I had learned that not long ago.

"At any rate, it didn't want to go on and destroyed itself. The land didn't feel good. The magic wasn't just gone, it was almost as if the enclave had been magically salted. There would be nothing more there. I heard the story, but it's the sort of the thing you don't expect to happen or to be involved with. Everything has gone smoothly for decades. I suppose we all got complacent."

She was right. People did get complacent. Perhaps I was, too.

My stomach was feeling more solid. I pushed myself up from the floor, taking a moment to stare at the toilet, giving myself a bit of time to settle.

Win rolled back into the main part of the bathroom. She waited while I washed up and rinsed my mouth. Together we went out to the main part of the library.

My arms began to tingle again, painfully so. The magic they were raising was definitely powerful. Lauren had joined them. Everyone held hands. The energy felt different. I could almost see a force field around the door extending out, probably around the entire section of the library building that held the conference rooms.

Lauren stumbled back and the chanting cut off. My arms stopped tingling, but the pain still ran up them, deep in my bones. I groaned. Win slumped over her rollator, no longer the vibrant old woman she had been. When she looked up, her face appeared even more lined and wizened than before.

Xavier bent down to cradle Lauren who seemed unresponsive.

"He's fighting back." Win drew in a deep breath and shakily rolled over to where Xavier knelt.

I followed, noting that even Bernice wasn't standing quite as straight as she normally did. Whatever had happened, it had been powerful. I hoped Lauren was okay. She would be the second friend I'd nearly lost in one day. And, of course, I may have lost my coworker Jack, even if I wasn't quite ready to call him a friend. Shuddering, I held my breath, hoping against hope that she'd be okay.

Chapter Eleven

A rotten stink began to permeate the library. It was an odor I'd come to associate with anything bad happening, rather as if bad magic literally stank. I wondered if others smelled it as well. Beneath that, Lauren's scent of cinnamon and rose reached me. She was on her side, crumpled down. Xavier had lifted her upper body in his arms and cradled her, rocking slightly.

He crooned ever so softly. To my knowledge he didn't have healing magic nor did he have a relationship with Lauren.

Randi stooped down as I got there and put a hand on Lauren's forehead.

She pulled it away, as if burned.

Bernice had pulled out a cell phone and was talking to someone.

"Is she alive?" I whispered.

Lucas looked over at me. "You can't tell?"

I shook my head.

"Then her spirit is in there," he said. "You know her well enough that she'd appear to you if she had died."

Xavier laid her back down. This time my arms tingled. He didn't do chest compressions, which I thought he might, but after a second of the tingling, Lauren gasped and spit and rolled over on her side, as if someone had done CPR.

I'd been the one to take first aid in my old office. I knew what to expect from someone who had had CPR done. Having it done magically probably didn't break ribs, which would be nice for Lauren.

"What?" she whispered, her voice more hoarse than normal. It seemed higher pitched, too.

"You were nearly dead," Xavier said. "We weren't sure, but Holly couldn't see your spirit nor could Lucas detect it in the room."

"There was a light, like they say," Lauren said. "And then I was back here."

Her voice was definitely pitched higher than usual. Even Lauren frowned, as if she heard it herself.

She ran her hands down her body, frowning even more. She started to say something and looked around at all of us, then closed her mouth.

"Casandra is on her way with a golf cart to take her over to the clinic. Ian is awake," Bernice said. "Dr. Mulrooney didn't want to leave him. She's afraid he'll get up and come investigate what's happening."

I half smiled, knowing Ian. He'd want to know everything that was going on.

"I'll go talk to him," I said.

Jeremy put a hand out and shook his head. "You stay with me or Randi. At all times. You can be across the room like you were, but you go nowhere alone. You're too vulnerable and while you have some abilities, you don't have as much training as I'd like to see in someone who's been targeted."

I swallowed and nodded. I hated not being able to go to Ian.

"I can go," Win said. She rolled up behind me. While I wouldn't ever think of her as being fast, she'd already turned her rollator around and was heading back. Her back bent over the rollator, though she held her head up. In shadow, she'd look like a hunchback.

"Win is probably the most powerful Innkeeper we have," Jeremy said quietly. "We're lucky she was willing to volunteer to come."

It could be difficult for Innkeepers to leave their enclaves but not impossible. They just didn't feel as powerful somewhere else. Win had said she could feel the power of our enclave, even if it wasn't hers. I'd been told that bringing something with them, rather like a vampire brings native earth, could help ground them, keep them more connected than they otherwise would be. I wondered if being telepathic, it was easier for Win to leave. She would, no doubt, have telepathic connections to certain people on her enclave.

Randi said nothing, just watched her go. "I still don't like it. What if the spirit has people here? More people than they've used to date. Win couldn't take a physical attack."

"Her spirit wouldn't give in. She doesn't want to stay here," Jeremy said. "I don't think I could take her one-on-one. She has enough magic on her own, not to mention the link to her own enclave. I suspect that the people there would all be willing to chip in magical energies to protect her, if she called."

That was something I hadn't realized an Innkeeper could do. Always something new to learn. I wondered how much Ian knew. He'd admitted he didn't know as much about his powers as he should. It was why Win had come.

She was supposed to teach him. But then he'd gone missing.

"Do you suppose the reason Ian was taken was to keep him from talking to Win?" I asked.

"That and keeping him from coming into more powers, yes," Xavier said. "I should go with her." He let Randi take over holding Lauren and stood up to hurry out.

I wondered if Xavier had a thing for Lauren. He'd been so concerned when she looked dead, crooning softly over her body, almost weeping. Plus, he'd been so gentle. Lauren hadn't said a word about it. Last I'd heard, she'd had a crush on Ian but nothing had come of it. Maybe she hadn't noticed Xavier's interest. Maybe it was a new thing.

Normally, I'd ask Ian, but who knew when I'd get to talk to him alone. I realized how much I relied on my friend to keep me informed and to have someone to talk to. It's not that I was lonely on the island. I talked to plenty of people, but Ian was my confidant. I missed him.

That left me with Jeremy, Randi, Lauren, Bernice, and Lucas. I stood, feeling awkward, as I had nothing to contribute. I didn't know enough about magic or my powers to try and use them. And everyone, including Win seemed to want to keep me from using them, as if that would immediately open me up to being possessed or influenced or something.

It wasn't long before Dr. Mulrooney's nurse, Casandra, arrived. She had a stretcher which she and Randi helped Lauren onto, though Lauren insisted she could walk. In moments, they were gone, Randi going with them.

Jeremy gestured to the table where we all sat down.

"Grant and whatever influenced him is sealed in the building. Unfortunately, we weren't able to get rid of the influence, so he has to stay there. The other enforcers will be here in the morning. I think one or two might catch the evening ferry and get here tonight. Until then, Holly, you stay with me. I don't want you doing any magic of any sort. Not even to light a candle beside your bed, do you understand?"

I nodded. I wasn't exactly in the habit of lighting candles beside my bed and if I were, I'd have used a match. My fire magic was far too powerful for candle lighting. Even under control, it was rather like trying to light a candle with a flamethrower.

"Lucas, I want you to keep an eye out for anything out of the ordinary. I have no doubt the spirit side has recruited Sharon. I know Holly saw her earlier. Sharon's energies could be one of the catalysts for all of this, though it seems to have built up even before Damien arrived. Someone should have noticed back then, but…" Jeremy shrugged, acknowledging that there wasn't much he could do about a mess left by U Council people long since dead.

Jeremy paced to the door and back. I felt the energy from his body, warm and fizzy like a live wire waiting to spark. He glanced over at me a few times. Nothing personal, though I could have wished for it.

Ian would have laughed at me. Once again, I wished for him to be there with me, holding my hand, even metaphorically, while island problems once again swirled around me.

"Do we know what happened to Jack?" I asked quietly when Jeremy stood near the table, staring out the main door.

Bernice didn't move, but gave me a long look, her arms crossed in front of her chest. Her eyes flicked over to Lucas, who shook his head before speaking.

"I suspect he's dead though they might have kept him alive for some reason. Win didn't sense him, either dead or alive. It's not impossible he got off the island on another boat before Xavier sent Kara to watch," Lucas said.

Jeremy put a hand to his forehead and leaned forward as if in pain. Lucas jumped up. Bernice took a step forward going to him. I followed the others, wondering what was going on.

"He's trying again to break the magical boundaries," Jeremy breathed. "I'll need help to reinforce them.

Lucas stepped over and placed a hand on Jeremy's shoulder and then one on his arm, helping him stand. Bernice held the other elbow, with a hand on his low back. I moved over. Jeremy's hand clasped mine, warm and solid and far too strong.

As he started the magic, my arms tingled and I felt the magic being pulled from my body so strongly, almost too strongly, causing me to double over. I struggled to breathe. Every time I lent magical support to someone, the experience got worse.

Chapter Twelve

The pain ended as quickly as it came. I stood up, feeling slightly dizzy. I put a hand on the solid oak of the library table where I'd been sitting, letting the feel of it, the hundreds of little ridges almost imperceptible beneath my fingers, ground me. I'd love to be like an oak, to be able to stand against whatever the strongest winds of fate threw at me.

The library once again had the faint scent of rotting meat that came with bad magic. Jeremy and Lucas were both breathing hard, though neither seemed to have felt the dizziness I had. The building was now silent, though I thought I remembered soft music playing in the background when I'd arrived.

"It's holding," Jeremy said, "But I don't like that he tried getting out. He's definitely connected to Jewel and can make trouble for everyone on the island."

"Should we evacuate?" Lucas asked.

"Hard to do," Jeremy said. "It's not like the other enclaves. Here, we'd need boats. And while we have the small ones for emergencies, we can't just commandeer a ferry."

Carl hurried in. "Xavier got to the clinic and sent me back here." He looked around at all of us.

"How is Ian?" Bernice asked before I could. I mentally thanked her for asking. I didn't want to sound like a broken record.

Carl smiled a little. "Less the worse for wear than I would have thought. I left him peppering Win with questions. I also made sure he understood he's not supposed to get up. He's supposed to rest. Something zapped a lot of his magic, sort of inundated one of the links to the island. It was a shock to his system, which is what knocked him out long enough to be put on a boat. It confused the island so that it didn't initially know what was happening."

"But I thought we said it was the island that did this." As usual, I was confused.

"No," Jeremy said. "It was part of the heart. We have the magic, which has its own sentience, but it doesn't understand us any more than we understand ants. Then there is the heart which formed the enclave. That was the heart or soul of a person who volunteered to anchor the magic to a place. They become a sort of interpreter of humans for the magic. But interpretation is always colored by experience. As bad things happen over centuries, even the most even tempered person can get cynical. In this case, not only did the living do horrible things, even the spirits attempted it. The magic knows the spirits who have remained and are less cynical, have become less controlled by their worst impulses, however it doesn't understand the conflicts. It's a blind elephant trying to get out of a China shop."

I wasn't sure I understood, but Lucas nodded along. "I

felt something when you reinforced the field around the conference room. He's angry. And rather self-pitying."

I wondered if the 'he' Lucas spoke of was Grant or if he meant Ambrose. At this point, it probably didn't matter.

Bernice snorted. "I wonder where he got the self-pity. It certainly wasn't part of Damien's makeup."

"We'll keep going through the histories," Jeremy said. He looked at me and I nodded. That would make me feel useful. My stomach growled loudly.

"But we'll need lunch first," Carl said. "But I doubt Lauren would appreciate us eating in the building."

"Reg is on his way," Bernice said. "He can cover the library while she's gone and do some of the reading. Are you staying here?" She looked at Jeremy.

"Holly needs food which means I'll need to leave. Can you stay?" Jeremy asked.

Bernice nodded. "I'm not sure I'm strong enough if he tries to break through again…

Jeremy shook his head. "Don't worry about it. I'll feel it. And this only has to last until tomorrow. Hopefully, he's tired."

I didn't think the heart of the island ever got tired, but perhaps it would be limited by what Grant's body could stand. My stomach growled again, reminding me I'd just had a huge amount of magical energy drawn from me. I always needed to eat after doing any sort of magic. It didn't matter that I hadn't actually done anything. Jeremy had used my energy. Now I needed to replenish.

When we left, I noticed that the day had stayed beautiful, the wind and rain of earlier only there to try and destroy the Innkeeper. It was the sort of day I'd normally hear birds singing on the island. Today, it remained quiet, not a single song bird around. It felt haunted.

When we got to the main road, I heard the waves

slapping against the shore, but still no birds. A bit of mournful sounding music came out of the grocery store. While it was getting late in the afternoon and I should have seen people walking up and down the street going home from work or getting food for dinner or even planning to grab an early dinner at Derry's, no one was around.

"It feels weird," I said quietly.

"Everyone feels the changes," Jeremy said. "Most don't know what it is, but they're listening to their gut and staying inside and quiet. No one wants to be noticed."

I didn't want to be noticed either, and when he pointed out that others were staying inside, I glanced up at the sky again, the clear blue with the fluffy clouds. I felt exposed. While I'd been hungry, now I felt vaguely nauseated like I was walking into the maw of a dragon.

While Jeremy didn't walk quite as fast as Bernice, he did keep a good pace and we arrived at Derry's before my imaginary dragon's maw could snap shut.

I stepped onto the stairs and was brought upstairs to the restaurant, which appeared like a diner today, though it didn't have the usual shine of a happy diner. The silver on the edges of the tables was scratched and scraped. The white laminate tops were dull. Even the red napkins looked over-washed and the chairs had a few rips here and there.

Normally, Derry's had plenty of people. That afternoon, I spotted only Kara in her wheelchair in a corner having lunch with a man I didn't know. He was very tall and very thin. I'd seen him around sometimes, but not often.

The violin music seemed to hit dissonant notes more often than not, as if it were a recording of a middle school orchestra instead of a professional one. Although, having heard one of my nieces playing in her school's orchestra, I could say that most middle schools played with more heart than the music in the background.

Gerald glowered at us and seated us near the door. He said nothing to me. Gerald had disliked me since I had dated Carl. Normally, he was at least polite, but today he was definitely out of sorts and not bothering to be polite. Not that he said much to Jeremy either. In fact, the glare he gave us made me wonder if he thought we'd done something wrong.

"No one seems like they're in a good mood, either," I said, keeping my voice low.

Mindy came out to take our order. She glared at Jeremy. I knew that most people in the enclaves were suspicious of enforcers, but I hadn't thought they'd be rude.

I ordered a burger and a small salad. I added a cup of their French onion soup, too, just because I wanted to treat myself. Jeremy ordered a cheesesteak sandwich, fries, salad, and a side of pot stickers, which didn't seem to go with his order, but Derry's could basically make anything.

"I wouldn't trust the pot stickers," Mindy said writing it down. "They aren't on the menu and the magic hasn't exactly been fast today. They might not be out first."

Jeremy nodded.

"I thought if Ian were back, things would be more normal for people," I said.

"I'm sure they are more normal, but more normal leaves room for a certain amount of strangeness. The diner isn't exactly perfect today, perhaps reflecting everyone's moods. The food will be slower, especially the stuff they've had to have magical help to create," Jeremy said. "Things are likely to deteriorate even more before tomorrow, when we can cleanse or replace the heart. The sentient buildings are part of the magic, though they are keyed as much to the person they have bonded with as they are with the heart. A cleansing is never easy for them, or their bonded human."

"Again, wouldn't it be safer if people left?" I asked.

Mindy brought out drinks and salads. She apologized again for the pot stickers not being ready. Jeremy waved her off.

"It might help the select few people who could leave, but it also leaves us with fewer people who create a sort of positive magical influence. Some of the change isn't as much about the heart as it is about people noticing the changes and being afraid or worried. Those folks may decide to leave the island. Don't be surprised if, when we leave here, you notice a fairly good-sized crowd at the dock."

I sipped my soda. The sugar immediately made me feel more grounded. However, it didn't stop me from devouring my salad, wishing I'd gotten a larger one. Mindy, however, brought out my French onion soup quickly enough that I didn't start growling. She also added in a basket of garlic bread, though neither of us had ordered it.

"It seems like you both were using magic, so we're throwing in some bread. Something's going on, isn't it? Ian's not been in to tell us a thing." Mindy seemed completely unaware of things I would have thought everyone knew. It appeared Ian was the main link in the chain of gossip. I also noted that in her quest for information, she'd stopped glaring at Jeremy every time she came to the table.

"Ian was injured," Jeremy said. "There'll be more enforcers arriving, hopefully on the next ferry."

Mindy's eyes widened at the news. She hurried off, probably to tell everyone in the kitchens what was happening. There weren't enough people in Derry's to have overheard, but I did see the couple at the other table turn to look at us in surprise.

"So you just tell folks?" I asked, between bites of soup. Jeremy had already taken some garlic bread.

He shrugged. "They'll find out. Besides, we like transparency, or as much as we can. Not everyone is ready to know everything about how magic works or how the enclaves are organized and such. So we tell residents what we can, what we know everyone will understand."

"It seems like the people I've met all either know more than I do or are asking the same questions." Which was true. Even people I didn't know well, like Kara, had the same type of observations.

"Maybe you bring out that side of them," Jeremy said. "People, even in the smallest enclaves, tend to fall into group patterns. It's not that anyone is trying to be cliquish, it's more that we're most comfortable with the people who see the world the way we do. For instance, Bernice thinks very highly of you and that's not a compliment she gives lightly. She's more at home with people who are self-sufficient so that tells me something about you. I suspect you also spend the most time with the other people on the island who tend to be self-sufficient. I'd be surprised if you knew Jack more than casually, as he is definitely not that way."

I laughed a bit, not a ha-ha but a surprised laugh because it was true about Jack. He needed things to be just so and he needed people to tell him exactly what they wanted and needed so he could offer that.

"Jack's probably dead, isn't he?" I said.

Jeremy looked sad. "Most likely. He could have just been sent off the island. People on land will look for him to make sure he wasn't sent off in a boat like Ian."

"Could other people on the island have had that happen to them, too?"

Just then Mindy came out with the rest of our meals. Except the pot stickers, which it looked like Jeremy would have for dessert. He didn't seem unduly upset.

He didn't answer until after Mindy had left. "It's not impossible. Hopefully, as Ian feels better and is more himself, he'll be able to tell us."

It sounded to me like we'd be going to see Ian after lunch. Which cheered me up more than it should have.

Chapter Thirteen

Lunch finished, finally, including Jeremy's pot stickers, we walked back down the hill towards the clinic. I was surprised at how happy that made me. Even clear, the skies were a glorious blue and no longer foreboding. While a light breeze still fluttered the leaves on the plants that grew in front of most of the buildings, it wasn't a chill breeze, just cool enough to keep the sun from feeling too warm.

I heard talking, which at first comforted me, but as we got closer to the dock, I noted that Jeremy had been right. At least two dozen folks stood around with bags, more bags than for an overnight trip to the mainland. Dirk and Bill both stood with their flannel shirts, sleeves rolled up, on the dock, army green duffels almost long enough to carry a human being, resting at their feet. Both men had back-packs as well.

It made me sad to see them there. I enjoyed their company and the certainty that on Thursdays when I went to the B&B for Eggs Benedict, I would see them. We'd exchange hellos. They weren't in the group of people that I counted on as friends, but we were friendly and they were people I liked seeing regularly. And now they were leaving.

I couldn't imagine either of them being fearful, yet here they were, waiting to leave the island.

My neighbor Sandra was there, too. She had a lot of her camera gear. She could have been going off island for work, though she usually told me when she was leaving. This seemed a bit more rushed. Just yesterday she'd returned, worried she wouldn't get back and now she was leaving.

Sandra saw me looking and waved me over. I paused, glancing at Jeremy. He nodded at me. I walked over to meet Sandra.

"You ought to come with me. Get off the island. Something is going on and I don't like it," she said.

"Yesterday you came back early…" I started.

Sandra shook her head. "I did. And this morning I felt the change. Things started to feel wrong. I'm surprised you can't tell, though you *are* new. This isn't the island I know."

I felt like she was patronizing me. I knew something was wrong. I also knew that I needed to stick around. That people who had hope, who were willing to see the good in the magic, could only help.

"I can't leave. Ian is here. And the cats…" I trailed off.

Sandra sighed. "The cats are part of the island. If something happens to them, the island is gone." She snapped her fingers.

I shuddered. I knew that about the cats. They were magic. But the idea of them just being gone, as if the island had sunk, was painful. There was nothing I could say, though my stomach turned slightly at the idea of losing them.

"As for Ian," Sandra continued, not noticing my reaction. "He's the Innkeeper."

Once again, I had this feeling that everyone knew things but me. I'd only heard the term Innkeeper for the first time in the last few weeks. No one had ever used it and now it seemed like people were throwing the term out all over the place in relationship to Ian. I was reminded of how once one decided on a certain model of car they seemed to be everywhere. Psychologists said it was because you were looking.

I couldn't be certain that was what was going on here. I'd have questioned the term "innkeeper" when I first heard it, so I hadn't heard it before I learned what it meant. Now it was everywhere. My hearing had not suddenly become better.

Jeremy waited a few steps away. I stepped back to go with him.

Sandra gave him the once-over, her eyes flicking from his head down to his feet. She smiled, then, almost knowing. "I'd stay for him, even if he does reek of council."

I laughed. I was staying for Jeremy, but not for the reasons she thought. I waved generally, getting waves from more than just Sandra. Dirk looked as if he wanted to say something, but then shook his head and gave a slightly larger wave.

Nodding at him, I turned to head back up the road. Jeremy had already turned to go towards the clinic. If anyone had any romantic ideas about the two of us, well, they'd probably learned differently right there. Even the most indifferent beau would have waited for me. At least I thought they would. Even my ex-husband would have waited.

The thought hit me with a certainty that my ex hadn't expected that I could keep up if he didn't go slow for me. He'd judged me based on my size and no matter what else I did, he determined that I, as a fat woman, couldn't have done certain things. A slow simmering anger bubbled up.

"Anger won't help," Jeremy said quietly. He hadn't slowed, but I had nearly caught up. He didn't turn around.

"It was just a stray thought," I said. A realization, actually, for exactly what sort of subtle disrespect I'd always settled for.

"The island pushes those buttons, makes you feel certain things. Keep it bottled up, whether you're attracted to Grant Arwen or whether you're angry at your ex." Jeremy's voice held no hint at what he thought of either of those things.

"Am I the only one on the island who doesn't read minds?" I asked.

"Win's the only telepathic one, but she linked to me on the ferry so that I could contact her if necessary." This time Jeremy turned around and grinned. "I felt your anger and asked her what was up. Win is every bit as much of a gossip as Ian. Sometimes I think it's a requirement for Innkeepers."

I hadn't exactly wanted to share my attraction to Grant with Jeremy. Nor did I like the idea that Win might have also ferreted out that I was attracted to Jeremy and possibly told him. I felt my cheeks burn at the thought.

Fortunately, Jeremy had already turned back to head towards the clinic. I followed a half-step behind him, mostly so that he didn't need to see the heat that had flooded my face and know that I was embarrassed. Unless, of course, Win had already let him know.

While I liked magic, telepathy was turning out to be something I most decidedly did not like.

The clinic was a two-story building beyond the library, hidden away behind some bushes and trees. The view out the windows tended to be all trees, especially from the beds on the second floor. I'd stayed there twice now, for short periods, and seeing only the trees was quite relaxing.

I couldn't say that I loved the outside of the clinic, which was rather sterile and plain with its white blocks and glass doors. Even the trim was only a cream color which blended into the white.

Jeremy waited for me, holding open one of the glass doors, though I didn't give him long to wait. As I grabbed the door my fingers brushed his and it seemed as if he let his hand linger a bit too long. Like I really needed another attraction to act on. Mentally I shook myself.

Fortunately, the moment my feet hit the black and white tile floors in the waiting area, I was reminded that Ian was there. And I was going to see him. That excitement drove everything else out of my mind.

Chapter Fourteen

Ian's room was on the second floor of the clinic. As I expected, upon entering, the view was of a bunch of trees. In fact, Ian was in the same room I'd stayed in the second time I was at the clinic. The floors were plainer in the rooms, a scuffed cream color, and everything smelled of disinfectant and sickness. Or at least the smell I associated with sickness.

Ian was in a bed, the head raised so he could talk. Win sat in the chair nearest the window and she smiled to see us, even though I knew she knew there wasn't a whole lot to smile about. Her rollator waited to one side, and she had a chair which was pulled up next to the bed.

As Jeremy and I entered the room, the area on our side of the bed became fuzzy before my eyes. I blinked and realized two empty chairs had appeared, one without arms, and one longer in the seat to accommodate Jeremy's height. The island knew. My arms hadn't tingled, so neither Ian nor Win had performed the magic. The island had done it, or the building did it the way Derry's would or the B&B.

Jeremy settled in the chair clearly meant for him and I sat in mine, leaning forward.

"I am so glad you're okay," I said, reaching for Ian's hand.

Ian reached out for mine and squeezed it, though the feeling was weak.

"I can't believe I was taken in," he said. His voice as a bit breathless and while he smiled, I could tell he felt tired. He was still recovering.

"I came to in the boat and had to use magic to keep it upright when the waves got high," Ian said. "I could feel the magic in the water, but couldn't grab onto the island's magic like I usually do. I had to rely on my own magic. The island is helping me heal, but it feels out of sorts."

Jeremy leaned forward and spoke. "Has Win explained why?"

Ian nodded.

"Can you sense Jack at all?" Jeremy asked him. "He seems to have been the trigger."

"I felt him when Holly came in to talk to Lucas," Ian said. "She left. Lucas left right after she did, like he was in a hurry. Didn't wave or anything. He felt almost blank, like something was blocking me or the B&B?"

Ian waited until Jeremy nodded that he understood. I didn't. Lucas had been cleared. Multiple times. The idea that he could have been influenced, or that he was one of the people who had helped harm Ian sent a chill down my back.

"Then something hit me. I tried to fight it, but I couldn't get a fix on who it was or what had happened. Everything went black until I came to in the little boat. It was a friggin' speed boat, for heaven's sake, and not much longer than I was, but there wasn't an engine. At least, not that I could find." Ian paused as if overcome by emotion.

His fingers grasped mine harder, not in a supportive squeeze but in the sort of squeeze that means someone is fighting pain. It took a few seconds before he could continue.

"By that time the waves were lapping over the sides and the thing was rocking around like crazy. I thought I was going to die out there when I couldn't communicate with the island. I couldn't even see it!"

I squeezed Ian's hand again, glad I hadn't let go. He glanced at me. I had tears at the corners of my eyes. Ian wiped a tear from his own. He'd been terrified. Even I could feel that. I wondered how Win, who was telepathic, and had probably picked up even more, could be so calm.

"Can you feel the people on the island now?" Jeremy asked.

Ian nodded.

"Is there anyone besides Jack who is missing? Someone you don't know why they're missing, as if they might have left on a boat while you were out?" Jeremy pressed.

Ian leaned back and closed his eyes. He disengaged his hand from mine, probably so he wouldn't inadvertently draw magic from me. Win, however, offered her hand and he took it. My arms tingled.

Letting out a breath, Ian opened his eyes and looked at me and then at Jeremy. He continued to hold Win's hand. His knuckles looked almost white.

"I don't feel Lucas, even though he should be here. It's like an empty spot where he should be. It's not like he's involved, but more like he died?"

Jeremy frowned and picked up his phone.

"I don't feel Gerald at all," Ian said.

"Gerald is here," Jeremy said, putting down the phone. "And Lucas is alive."

He stood up, walking over to the door. I stayed seated

near Ian, hoping that maybe Jeremy would let me stay with Win and Ian. I mean, two Innkeepers, even if one wasn't at full power should protect me.

"Holly," Jeremy said, his voice had the edge of an order to it.

I sighed and stood. "Two innkeepers?" I asked, hoping he'd realize I would be safe.

Jeremy shook his head. "If something has happened to Lucas, I'm going to need your powers. I don't have enough spirit magic. If I have to confront Lucas, I need someone who can help."

I stood up. At least I could be useful even though I hated leaving Ian behind. He gave me a small smile and waggled four fingers at me. I gave him an equally small wave as we left the room.

It was harder to go than I thought. It felt like leaving everything I knew that was safe about the island. Standing in the hallway with Jeremy, I felt exposed, just as I had when we first walked up the road. I wondered if it was possible for someone to spy telepathically.

Chapter Fifteen

I followed Jeremy back to the library. We'd not been in the clinic for long, but the day already seemed to be slipping away. The sun was just low enough to make me think of evening. Fog was rising, which meant that either someone was doing magic or the ferry was nearly there. So far the mist only danced around my ankles, so I could see perfectly well.

I smelled dampness and a citrusy spice that seemed to come from Jeremy as he waited for me to walk beside him, instead of marching off into the fog, leaving me to follow. I wasn't sure if he waited for me because he worried that I'd be killed or incapacitated if he didn't, or if he didn't trust me not to run back to Ian and Win.

"At least the ferry is nearly here. There are two more enforcers on it. Once I link up with them, you'll be able to spend some time with Ian and Win," he said quietly.

I was thankful that he at least understood how much I wanted to spend more time with Ian, how worried I'd been about my friend. I hadn't even given Ian a hug, but he hadn't seemed receptive to one, although that's not really like him. Still, I'd never run into him in a hospital room. Knowing him, he'd whine about how pale he was—true—and how horrible hospital gowns bleached him out—also true—and then wonder if I thought he looked as horrible as he thought he did. Which totally wasn't true and hopefully mind-reader Win would let him know.

The library felt empty. It wasn't, of course. Bernice was there along with Xavier, Carl, and Lucas, although Lucas was sitting oddly. I could feel the faintest tingle of magic on my arms. Sharon had told me it was a common reaction and I'd get used to it, but it still bothered me more than it seemed to bother other people. I couldn't imagine that other people just ignored the sensation when it got stronger, which made me wonder if Sharon had lied or if, perhaps, I was more sensitive than most to various magical workings.

Bernice and Xavier looked up and saw us. Randi came out from behind the stairwell and looked at us.

"I'll go get food," she said upon seeing Jeremy. He nodded at her and she turned to go. She must have left the hospital before we got there, or maybe she'd been in Lauren's room.

"How is Lauren?" I asked.

"She's holding on," Randi said shortly, as she walked out the door.

When we got closer, I noted that Xavier looked more haggard than usual. Lines etched his face where before they'd been subtly drawn. Even the sharpness of his eyes seemed diminished.

"The fog is coming in," Jeremy said. "We'll have some help soon."

Xavier gave a slight tilt of his chin to indicate he'd

heard. Bernice turned from us and stared at the door to the conference rooms.

Jeremy indicated I could sit in one of the chairs, though the one he pointed at was as far from Lucas as it could be.

"Is anyone going after Gerald?" Jeremy asked Xavier.

"I don't have the manpower," Xavier sighed. "Carl and I were both here trying to subdue Lucas. He must have known when you talked to Ian …"

"Interesting." Jeremy rubbed his chin with a hand, an almost cliché look that suggested he was thinking.

"He's linked to the island spirits," Bernice said. "For good or ill. Whatever was in him, picked up what was happening at the clinic and decided to attempt to remove us. Whatever is possessing Grant hit the magical barrier hard at the same time."

Jeremy sighed. While he'd always seemed so in charge, suddenly he looked a bit defeated, as if there was too much going on. I couldn't blame him. There was a lot. And it seemed like the moment we got rid of one problem, others cropped up, like weeds. Maybe he was right. Maybe we needed to start over on the island, but I couldn't imagine anyone being willing to offer their life as a sacrifice.

"Are you okay?" I asked Carl. He dated Gerald. It must be hard to find out that someone you loved had been taken over, or worse, was voluntarily helping.

"There's a reason Gerald and I have a rather dramatic relationship," Carl said. "You weren't the first person he scared off. It was always just easier to give in to him. The seeds were always there. I'm not sure he's been taken over."

Carl didn't look at me when he said that. His chest looked almost caved in, protecting a pain or hurt that he didn't want to share. Though he might attempt to hide it, the pain was too great for complete success.

"Gerald was always borderline for being investigated by someone like Grant," Bernice said. "He wasn't like Lucas or even Jack."

Her expression didn't change, but something sad passed behind her eyes.

"No one should think they missed something," Jeremy said glancing around at all of us. "Every enclave thinks the best of their people. Jewel's issues no doubt started out as small pockets of negativity of the sort everyone has, an argument here or there, a petty squabble that amounts to nothing, but as time went on the island couldn't discharge it any longer. It happens. There's a human at the heart of every island. Sometimes the wrong thing happens at the wrong time and the outlook changes. Then it feeds off the negativity. Someone like Gerald, who might tend towards negativity, becomes worse, which makes the island worse. With Damien… well, an already faltering heart never had a chance."

Beyond the windows, the long narrow ones that allowed Lauren to see outside, something she appreciated about the building, I noticed the fog had completely rolled in. Jeremy glanced up.

"The ferry should be here," he said. "Anyone want to help me?"

He pulled on Lucas's arm and made him stand. Xavier and Carl moved to help. Bernice stayed where she was.

"Call Rose. She can help hold the barrier," Xavier said, looking at Bernice. Bernice had her phone out before he'd stopped speaking.

The three men took Lucas with them. I wasn't sure whether to stay where I was or go with them.

"Holly," Jeremy said. "Randi should be back in a few

moments. Remain with Bernice, but don't get too close to the barrier. Whatever you do, don't lend her any of your strength. We haven't figured out how Lucas was influenced."

I remained at the table while Bernice talked to Rose. Randi arrived moments later with several bags that all said Derry's on them. She waited while the men disappeared and then set down her stuff on the table near me.

"Bernice, you haven't eaten," she said, pulling out a container with a large sandwich and some fries. In another bag, she had sodas, more than one for each person.

"Lauren will hate that we're eating in here," Bernice said, eyeing the window as if she were thinking of being polite and taking her food outside.

"Stay away from the books," Randi said. She moved the pile of old books we'd been searching through earlier to an adjacent table. "It should be fine."

I wasn't hungry, so I didn't take anything. Randi offered me a soda. I declined. She and Bernice ate with the same ravenous hunger I'd experienced earlier. At least this time, I wasn't so depleted I needed to eat every few minutes.

Randi attempted to make small talk, but I was distracted. The magic from the door kept drawing my attention. I couldn't figure out why. I didn't feel any tingling in my arms, but there was something about the barrier that wasn't quite right.

Bernice, of course, rarely made small talk. She spoke if she had something to say. At that point, she was clearly hungry, wolfing down the food that Randi had brought.

I wished, suddenly, that Jeremy hadn't left me with Randi. That I had gone with him to the docks to meet the new enforcers and escort them here.

"Who are the enforcers on the ferry?" I asked Randi.

"Jeanine Callahan," Randi said between bites of fries. "And her partner, Elena Rodriguez."

"I've met Elena," Bernice said. "And heard about Jeanine. She's second to Jeremy, isn't she?"

"She's a better team player than Jeremy, so in some circles they prefer her. But yeah, Jeremy has more power and he's not afraid to use it," Randi said. "I've been paired with him as an observer probably a dozen times now. I prefer working with Jeanine and Elena, though. Easier to talk to. Gentler in terms of their approach."

"Jeremy gets the job done," Bernice said. She held an onion ring for a moment, studying in and then bit off a piece.

I placed a hand over my mouth to hide a smile. The same could be said of Bernice. She got the job done, although she probably wouldn't be anyone's favorite. She'd grown on me, though, and I'd miss her if she were gone.

Randi said nothing and went back to her sandwich.

"Will the three of them be enough to keep the negativity from spreading?" I asked.

"They'll try." Randi looked down at her food, trying to decide what to eat next. "I doubt they'll be able to clear the darkness, unfortunately. Jewel is going to need another heart."

"How will they choose who it is?" I asked. The door behind me opened and I looked back, expecting to see Jeremy and the others, but Rose entered slowly, barely avoiding being hit by the interior door as it closed. She wobbled along, slowly, her head bobbing up and down.

"Someone will volunteer," Randi said. "Someone always does."

"It seems so medieval." I couldn't help but remember horror movie premises where someone is drugged into thinking they were volunteering to be sacrificed when they weren't volunteering at all. I worried about Win.

"I don't like that barrier," Rose said. Her voice was stronger than her body appeared to be.

"It's fine," Randi said. "I checked it a few minutes ago when I got back with food."

Rose shook her head. "I can see it. It's fraying already."

Bernice stood, half-closing her eyes. I felt my arms tingle. Rose could clearly see magic, just as I felt its tingle.

"It's definitely fraying," Bernice said. "I'm not sure the fraying is new, either. I can't believe we missed it."

"He wants you to," Rose said. She looked over at me. "I don't like that Holly is here."

"She has to stay," Randi said. "She has to remain with either me or Jeremy."

"Probably a man's idea," Rose snorted. I hadn't heard her snort, before. In fact, I'd rarely heard her speak. Usually just a yes or a no, as if the very act of speaking was work.

Bernice nearly smiled which made me smile a bit.

"But if the barrier is fraying..." I trailed off not sure what that meant. I could feel something wrong from the door, but I couldn't see it the way Rose could.

Rose patted my shoulder. "I'm sure the men know better." Her voice already sounded less strong and the patting was so light it might have been a breeze.

Randi rolled her eyes. "They should be back in a few with along with Jeanine and Elena."

Rose smiled. "Jeanine started here, did know that?" She looked towards Bernice, though with her bobbing head she took in all of us.

"She left before I arrived, but I heard about her from Elena," Bernice said. Both she and Randi continued eating, as if fixing the fraying barrier wasn't an issue.

Rose reached out a shaking hand and took one of the extra cans of soda and pulled the tab. She grinned, or at least I thought she did as her head bobbed towards the can. I worried it wouldn't make it to her mouth, but her hand shook in time to her head bobbing and she finally managed a sip.

The temperature in the room plunged. My first thought was a ghost. Still, nothing appeared to me. It was like what had happened earlier when I'd thought I had seen Sharon. I couldn't believe all this had happened in just one day. My body felt heavy and tired at the very thought.

I shivered.

Randi shivered, too. Bernice sat stoically, before she stood and turned towards the barrier.

"He's using ice to push the barrier," Bernice said.

Rose pushed herself upright, slowly as always.

My arms began to tingle.

The chill dissipated and something moved through me like a warm breeze. Magic.

My arms ached and itched. I breathed through the pain. Randi straightened to her full height, both hands out, palms facing the door.

An ache started at the top of my head. I remembered that when a spirit had tried to possess me, I'd felt something similar. I concentrated on pushing it away, thinking the words "go away" while using my magic to create a shield against whatever it was.

The ache turned into a hammering. I didn't understand why I wasn't cold any longer. My eyes closed against the pain.

Someone touched my arm. My stomach flipped and I thought for a moment I would vomit, but the food stayed down. My head still hurt, but the hammering had stopped. The ache felt like the aftermath of the pounding I'd endured. I breathed in, though my body felt tired.

Without thinking about it, I laid my head down in my hands and willed myself into unconsciousness.

Chapter Sixteen

I smelled citrus and spice before I opened my eyes. I felt the warmth of people standing around me. My headache was gone. I listened as people whispered. I wondered how long I'd been out.

"She's coming around," an unfamiliar voice said.

I pushed my head up and opened my eyes. A woman with waves of lightly curling black hair knelt next to me, touching my thigh. Her large dark eyes looked tired, or maybe they were worried. I didn't know her. Her skin was bronze and lightly lined, but so soft looking my hands ached to reach out and rub her cheek.

Jeremy sat on my other side. Rose stood closest to the door, head bobbing and hands shaking, perhaps chanting a spell against whatever was happening. Randi stood with her. Bernice was on the other side of the table watching me carefully, eyes half-closed the way they often were when she did magic.

Surprisingly, though everyone appeared to be doing magic, my arms weren't tingling.

I looked around. Behind the woman who spoke, an

older white woman stood. She was tall and thin, and in the right movie she could have played Hera or one of the other goddesses of the hearth. Her gray hair was pulled back in a single braid which she'd wrapped around her head. She wore jeans and a rainbow t-shirt with the slogan "Grandma does it with Pride."

"What happened?" The older woman asked.

"I don't know," I said. "My head started to hurt. Then it felt as if someone was hammering at it. I was worried something was trying to possess me. It had happened like that once before, so I concentrated on sending whatever it was away. After that, I felt really weak."

"You got rid of him. Good." The woman next to me spoke. The alto of her voice held an almost singsong tone to it as she spoke.

Jeremy touched my wrist lightly, taking my pulse. He nodded to himself.

"She ate not long ago, and her pulses are strong. The weakness had to be magical. I suspect that Grant was sent out to attempt to siphon some of her magic."

"She doesn't feel particularly weak magically," the woman next to me said.

"You should feel her magic at full power," Jeremy said quietly, nodding approvingly.

The other two raised eyebrows, but said nothing.

"I'm Elena," the woman next to me said. Which meant the woman behind her had to be Jeanine. "I'd like to try a visioning into your mind to see if I can track what happened. Also, with your magic, as you have spirit magic, you might have picked up some information we can use, even if you don't know it."

I nodded.

Jeremy's hand tightened slightly, still resting on my wrist as if he were continuing to take my pulse.

I became aware of him in a way I hadn't been aware before. Part of me wanted to lean back against him, but I resisted the impulse. He was an enforcer. He was only appreciating the power of my magic.

"A visioning isn't always pleasant," Elena said. "It will feel as if I'm slamming my body into yours. The stronger your magic, the harder the wall, it seems. Just keep focusing on your breath. I'll see what happened and hopefully trace the source. You might feel some of the achiness of the head pain you experienced earlier, but it shouldn't be as bad as it was the first time. Okay?"

I nodded.

Elena stood up. After a moment she placed both her hands on my shoulders, pushing me deeper into my chair. I let my eyes close. Jeremy removed his hand from my wrist. I wished he'd continued to touch me. His hands were warm, and without his touch, I realized just how cold I felt.

Soon enough I felt the slam Elena mentioned. It was so strong I felt my body being pushed further back into my chair.

I had a vision of someone straddling me, trying to strangle me. For an instant I couldn't breathe. I focused. After a moment, my lungs began to work again.

My scalp tingled. There was a hint of an ache, but more a memory of one than the pain I'd felt just a few minutes ago. Or maybe it had been longer than that. I wasn't certain. After all, I'd been out and hadn't checked a clock.

Breathing became difficult, once again forcing me to focus on my body and my breath.

I had an image of Sharon. Deep down I knew she'd been involved in whatever had happened. I thought I glimpsed Grant Arwen flailing around in a dark pool at the edges of my vision, barely staying above water, hands waving.

Then, without warning, the pressure on my body was gone. I could fill my lungs more easily.

I opened my eyes.

"Interesting," Elena said quietly.

"What?" Jeremy and Jeanine asked at the same time.

"An older woman, I think Sharon?" Elena asked.

I nodded, knowing who she meant. "Probably. I think I saw her while you were doing the visioning."

"She was leading, being pushed by a shadow of a person. I saw the shadow being eaten away by something I didn't see. I think that Sharon has been doing what she can to influence the heart."

"But how can a spirit do that?" I asked.

"The heart was already compromised. I suspect that when Damien Bane was here he influenced the heart to be more receptive to Sharon. The pure magic rejects as much negativity as it can understand, but the heart, well, the heart was once human. And we all tire. Immortality as an enclave is not for the weak," Elena said in her singsong voice.

"Is she still here?" I whispered, realizing that I had only my own impressions that I'd managed to fend off the spirit.

Elena shook her head. "You managed to fight her off with some help from the magic. There's a tie to you, though I'm not sure what it is."

I suspected it was because my ancestor had been killed on the island before she became bonded to it. When I'd arrived, she'd reached out to me to cut that tie. After doing that, I'd helped banish Damien and inadvertently killed Sharon. No doubt whatever goodness was left in the magic appreciated that.

"The enclave, then, is not completely darkened," Jeremy whispered. "There's a chance?"

I hoped he meant there was a chance no one would have to be sacrificed.

"It feels too weak, to me," Jeanine said finally. "We'll need a new one. We have some time, but if Grant keeps fighting, we won't."

"I saw him," I said, since Elena hadn't mentioned it. "During Elena's visioning. I saw Sharon and I saw Grant. Grant was in the background and he was like a man drowning in a black pool, flailing his arms around."

It almost hurt to remember. There had been something desperate in those moves.

"It's sucking him dry," Elena said. "Poor Grant. He was one of our best."

"Can't you help him?" I asked. I remembered the look, the instant attraction. Not that I wasn't also attracted to Jeremy. But the moment with Grant had been instantaneous. Maybe it was just a spell to keep me off my game, but I remembered that feeling.

"We can try," Jeanine said. "But we all know the dangers. Whether we're successful depends upon exactly what we find in there."

"I had hoped to wait until tomorrow," Jeremy said.

"It would be best," Elena replied. "There are only three of us. We could do it, but it would be exhausting."

"Randi can back us up. I've worked plenty of cases with only a watcher as my backup." Jeremy said it with almost a growl. Confidence that bordered on arrogance.

"We should wait," Jeanine said. "Even if it means losing Grant. It's the recommended path."

"Not for Grant," Jeremy replied quietly. He glanced at Rose.

"Who would volunteer?" Elena asked. "Have you talked with anyone? Is there anyone in the clinic?"

"I'll send Randi to talk to the enclave physician to see," Jeremy said.

"So many people left earlier," Jeanine added. "I hope that whoever would be the best choice didn't leave."

The *best choice* made it sound less than voluntary, but I said nothing. I'd already asked, and been answered. Suddenly, like always, I felt powerless. Jeremy and Rose and everyone else might talk about my level of power, but that was only matched by my lack of understanding. It was hard to feel powerful when you didn't understand your power or what you could do with it.

It occurred to me that perhaps Jeremy was buttering me up in hopes that I would volunteer to be the next sacrifice. Maybe if I were attracted to him enough I'd volunteer to be the next heart. I liked him and all, but I wasn't that interested. I dug in, reminding myself of all the reasons I wanted to live.

Chapter Seventeen

I sank into a funk, worried that I was being played. Again. I mean, my history with my ex was such that I tended to listen, to take people at face value, only to be hurt. I'd stayed with my ex for nearly twenty years while he'd talked about waiting to start a family until we had a better nest egg, a larger house, until the company, which his father owned, was on better footing and so on. I'd listened. I'd waited.

When I was nearly forty and starting to push for the child because my body would soon become physically incapable of becoming pregnant, he'd told me he'd met someone else.

And she was pregnant with their child.

She was younger, prettier, smaller than me.

It had been a huge blow to my self-confidence which had always been shaky thanks to having been, what my parents euphemistically called, "a big girl" since I was a youngster. My sisters were stocky, but wore straight sizes and had never had the embarrassment of having to shop in the plus-sized departments as I had always done.

By high school, I'd become large enough that even plus-sized departments hadn't always carried my sizes. As an adult, I'd found that even the fat girl stores often didn't have sizes for me in stock and I was relegated to ordering clothing. While my choices had expanded in the last few years with online shopping, my choices to try things on hadn't.

I'd finally come to terms with my size. I took pride in the things I could do and in the things my body did for me. Even at the lowest point of my life, when I'd been struggling to find a job, I'd come to accept that I was who I was and I looked how I looked. Given that I was pushing against what the culture thought of as attractive and even "healthy," it hadn't been easy and my self-acceptance had its ups and downs.

Now, here I was, looking at not one but two very handsome men and fantasizing that they might be interested in me. Maybe Grant Arwen had been himself when he eyed me, but perhaps that had just been a spell. Jeremy seemed more interested in me now than he had when he'd first come to the island. But perhaps he was just hoping that if I liked him, I'd agree to volunteer to be the island's next heart. After all, one thing they needed was someone with a lot of magic. I'd been told I was extremely powerful on more than one occasion.

I was roused from my funk by the sound of the library doors opening. So far as I knew, everyone was already here. But I broke into a smile when I saw Ian sashaying across the room with Win pushing her rollator along behind.

While Ian looked a bit pale, his eyes too large in his face, he looked more himself than he had been earlier at the clinic.

"Ian!" I said standing up and heading to him.

Jeanine put a hand on my arm, holding me back.

"Oh let her come!" Ian said. "I'm fine. I can take a hug from one of my besties!"

I noted Win's nod from behind him. Only then did Jeanine let me go. Ian was as tall as I was, though he was much thinner. He hugged me so hard I worried I'd smoother him.

When he stepped back, I noted he wore a pair of purple plaid flannel pajama bottoms. He had on a black long-sleeve t-shirt over the top, with a square of purple plaid on it. I wondered if those were lounging pajamas. They were certainly different than his typical daily black jeans and vest.

He had on black high-topped tennis shoes.

"I'm glad to see you," I said, my voice low.

"Win's been keeping me appraised of what she knows. Did you know she can telepathically link to others? And she knows what Jeremy knows," Ian whispered. "I figured you could use an ally here."

I glanced back at the others. Win had come up and pushed her way past us. Jeanine and Elena were greeting her. The others stood around the table, perhaps out of ear shot if I didn't talk too loudly.

"Do you think…" I trailed off, about to ask Ian if he thought I was being groomed to be the next heart, when Jeremy joined us and looked Ian up and down. My arms tingled. He was too close for me to finish my sentence without him overhearing.

"I think a lot," Ian hissed back, smiling. He clearly had no idea of my worries. I hoped that Win wouldn't tell on me. Her telepathy made me uncomfortable, particularly if I wasn't supposed to know they wanted me for the heart.

We all walked towards the table. Ian pointedly ignored Jeremy who was clearly trying to see if there were any issues remaining.

"He's clean," Win said. She sat down at the table, taking my seat. "It's good you removed Lucas. He's very much influenced. I think he might even have been possessed."

"Is he a threat to people off the island?" I asked.

"We came with Derek," Elena said. "He might just be a watcher, but he's powerful. He'll keep an eye on him until there are enough enforcers to deal with him. Derek knows that waiting for reinforcement is important, when it can be done."

"That's where we differ," Jeremy responded, aware that he was being criticized. "I don't think we have time. Already one of the most powerful spirit magic mages has been influenced. Grant Arwen, another council-trained mage was influenced and is being used against us. How many more?"

Elena sighed.

"The barrier is better," Rose said as she came over to the table. She put her hands on the top, leaning on them, making them shake slightly, her head bobbing with her words. Then she slowly lowered the rest of her body to a chair. Her movements seemed to take forever. I wondered what it was like to have a mind like hers, to have the power that she appeared to have, but have a body that struggled even to sit down.

Randi said nothing. She stood off to the side, watching all of us, arms crossed over her chest.

Bernice sat beside Xavier. Carl stood behind them, leaning against one of the other tables. He, too, seemed to be a watcher. I wondered if we were being guarded.

"Win is strong enough to help us," Jeremy said quietly.

Win nodded. "I know the spells."

"I can hold," Ian said. "Win explained to me what would happen."

"Your link was recently severed…" Jeanine said quietly.

"Win helped me reset it. She explained what would happen if we needed a new heart. I focused on linking to the magic itself rather than through the heart. I can hold," Ian reiterated. He glanced at me. "The magic will help me do it."

"I think Ian could need help. I'd feel better with Win backing him up. That would leave us two short of the people we'd need," Jeanine said.

"I know the spells," Bernice said. "I can help so long as I don't take an active role."

"Randi could be the fifth," Jeremy said quietly. "Xavier and Carl can observe. They're both strong enough."

Xavier lowered his head in agreement. "I would need a quick education on what I need to watch for."

"I could do that. Give me an hour with him?" Randi looked over at Jeremy.

"That will give me time to find the volunteer," he said.

"You already know who you'll pick," Elena said. "We just need to hear her say it."

My heart sank. I thought I was going to vomit. They really did think I was going to volunteer to be the next heart of the island. I didn't want to die. I had no desire to die.

Win reached over and patted my hand. She shook her head slightly as if encouraging me to refuse the position.

Rose sighed. "What are the words?" she asked.

"Say that you chose of your own free will to become the heart of the enclave," Jeremy said. "That none of us are coercing you."

Rose repeated the words, her voice shaking slightly along with her head.

"And why do you make this choice?" Elena asked, her voice kind.

"I make this choice because I'm old. I can smell death just around the corner," Rose said. "I've had palsies and strokes and any number of issues for the last two decades. I've pushed through and lived the life I could, but my will is tiring. I kept fighting because I love Jewel and didn't want to leave it, even in death. It was the place that gave me work and a life of meaning in these last years. I didn't... I *don't* want to lose it. I love the people here. I've loved my job..."

I felt tears coming to the corners of my eyes even as Rose choked a bit. Jeanine handed her a bottle of water from the stash of food and drink Randi had brought earlier.

"I'd love a margarita from Derry's," Rose said. "My liver wouldn't take alcohol, even here, for the last years. I remember once on a trip to Mexico, I had the best one with my husband. Can you tell them that?"

Elena nodded and stood. "I'll go bring one over."

Ian closed his eyes and focused. I felt more of a tremble in my legs than a tingle in my arms. I wasn't sure what he was doing, but then he looked up.

"Derrys'll be able to make it perfectly, now," he said.

Win gave him a serene smile. She caught my eye and winked as if to say she told me so.

I didn't know Rose well. I'd often been annoyed by her slowness and the way she moved. But the idea of losing her was a gut punch. Particularly to lose her this way. I still wondered what had happened to Jack. Win thought he was probably dead. I hoped, though, that she was wrong. Maybe someone would find him.

Elena left.

Rose sat confidently at the table. I wouldn't have been so confident and serene if I were her.

"What happens next?" I asked, looking around.

"I'll hold the island together with Win's help while the other five destroy the old heart and then create the new one," Ian said, as if it were that easy.

"We'll need to go down to the caverns where the heart was first created, or at least be close. It's also where Damien made his sacrifices, which isn't ideal, though," Bernice added. She didn't look at all troubled about Rose dying, though she had reached over to touch Rose's hand.

Jeremy pressed his hands together, leaning forward. "We should have noticed that sooner. But none of us has had to go through the re-hearting of an enclave. We've been able to save others."

I wondered how many had had to be saved.

Jeanine looked down at her hands. "I was nearly killed once, saving an enclave. The heart reached out to try and take someone…"

"We know that this one has been changed beyond repair," Jeremy said. "You'll have more protection."

"From who? You've already put Carl and Xavier on watch." Jeanine asked. "Who else would know the spells?"

"David knows them," Carl said. "He can watch and I can protect."

Jeremy nodded at him. Carl left to find David. He had his cell phone, but perhaps he worried that David wouldn't immediately pick up.

"What will I be doing?" I asked. "I'm not supposed to be alone, but…" Everyone else had a part. I had nothing.

Jeremy sighed. "I hate having you there, but I hate leaving you on your own more." He looked around at Jeanine. His eyes didn't quite meet hers.

"Ideally, we'd call the ferry and get you off the island, first," Jeanine said to me. "But, again, someone is in a hurry."

"We could need her," Bernice said. "Holly has a lot of power and she's used to sharing it."

Jeremy nodded. "It's frighteningly easy to draw power from her. Even for me. Her pool of abilities seems almost infinite."

Win stood and pulled out her rollator. Ian started to join her, but she waved him off.

"Come with me, Holly. We're going to get you set up with more protection spells and the ability to feed people your energy without letting them take too much." Win moved her rollator across the library to the other side.

I stood and followed her, glancing back once at Ian, who shrugged and watched me go.

Chapter Eighteen

Win led me across the library. We could still see the others, but were out of ear shot. Xavier and Randi were the furthest from us, though I felt occasional tingles of magic on my arms.

Further from the barrier, I smelled the usual library smells of paper and dust. No matter how much magical housekeeping went on, that many books, that much paper always accumulated dust. Not so much that I needed to sneeze, but still… dust. Traces of Lauren's perfume lingered and I hoped she was doing well. The last few months had been hard on her. She'd been injured just a month ago, perhaps because she knew too much. This time she'd been injured trying to protect her library.

While I could hear the other people, I could only hear murmurs of conversation. I wondered what everyone was talking about. Ian seemed keen on what Jeremy was saying.

Win settled and patted my hand. "Come now. You already know some basic protection spells. I want you to enhance them further. Think of it as using those on the spirit level and then also the physical and mental level."

I drew in a breath and focused on doing one of the protection spells that Bernice had taught me. I wasn't sure about the levels, but I tried to expand it outward, thinking that might work.

Win shook her head. "No. Think about going deeper. Keep it where it is, but send it higher and lower in your mind. At least that's the imagery I catch from you about the levels."

I tried.

Win frowned.

I wasn't quite getting it.

She went back and forth with me, trying to give me an image I could utilize. We finally found something I could do.

"Now, I need to give you an off switch for when you share your magic with another. Before you lay a hand on anyone, I want you to think of your magic as going through a faucet. You have the ability to let it all out, with the faucet fully opened or you can also close the faucet off to nothing or a mere trickle. Don't open it fully while we're working. You'll exhaust yourself too quickly, particularly for what's coming," Win said.

"How long will this take?" I asked. "How is it that Rose can be killed when the island protects us against death?"

"She will talk to the magic about it and the magic will accept her offer. She doesn't die, per se. Her body will cease, but the essence of Rose will continue here," Win said. "No one knew the old heart, so no one had a name. For now, everyone will think of Rose as the heart and call her by that name, probably for a decade at least. As Innkeeper, Ian will be the last to go and once he's gone, she will just be the heart. But she'll continue, though the longer she's gone the less personal her senses will be. And of course, as Ian winds down, getting closer to dying, he'll be less human too, just as I can feel myself becoming less and less the woman I once was."

Win seemed completely warm and human to me. I couldn't imagine her any other way than the way she was.

"I wasn't nearly so warm then," Win said. "And my telepathy is a fraction of what it was. One of the other Innkeepers thinks that's what keeps me more human than many Innkeepers at my age."

"I had no idea. But, talking about Rose, I won't have to stand there and watch someone plunge a knife into her chest or anything?" I did watch too many movies and I really didn't want to have the image of Jeremy in white robes holding a knife over her chest in my head.

Win smiled. "I've seen those movies, too. But no. That's not how we work. Rose will give herself to the island. There are words that will be said. She'll have them written out for her and if her desire is pure and true and she is not being coerced, the magic will take her. If my enclave needed a new heart, I would be tempted. I've heard it's a peaceful way to go, though I could be wrong."

"Even so, it's strange enough to think the island has a consciousness that wasn't like ours. It's even weirder to think that it might have a human consciousness too," I said.

"But Rose won't be human any longer, will she? Our consciousness changes after death. Even the spirits that inhabit the island are not quite what they once were. Sharon will be banished in the ceremony, as well any spirit that harbors negative energy. But even if Sharon wasn't banished, eventually she'd lose interest in trying to possess someone because she wouldn't understand why she wanted a body any longer. She'd be used to being a spirit and having that freedom. It's why the newly dead are always the most dangerous."

It all made sense.

"I wish Bernice answered questions like you do," I said. "I feel like I'd have been more equipped to deal with the stuff going on."

"Bernice is brilliant," Win said, glancing at our mayor wistfully. "I wish she fully understood just how brilliant she is. I think that would have made her a more generous teacher. There's a reason she was the one the U Council attempted to have infiltrate the enclave when Damien was here."

"How did they not know he was older than he should be?" I asked.

"Some people have a healing magic that keeps them young. I've known a few who live to be nearly two centuries old before they get tired and die. It's not unheard of. And it's only been recently that the enclaves were as connected. The council always existed, but because people couldn't easily communicate, they couldn't check things out very quickly. Damien was smart about what he did. He slowly pushed his influence onto the residents, so no one ever complained. No complaints meant there was no reason for an enforcer, who would have noticed, to come to Jewel. And, when they did, they were focused on someone else."

"How do people become enforcers?" I asked, keeping my voice low. "I mean when Jeremy and Randi were first here, people were really unsure about them. It was almost like they dreaded and hated having them here."

"For Xavier, it could be like the FBI coming in and claiming jurisdiction. There are always politics. Add to that, enforcers are above island law. Any of them, even Randi, could go on a murderous rampage and Xavier couldn't do a thing about it except call the council and have them send more enforcers," Win explained. "So things could go bad very quickly."

"Has it ever happened?" I asked.

"Enforcers go through a lot of training. They also have telepaths like me go through their memories, their wants, even their most buried desires to see if they can handle the responsibilities. No one is perfect, of course, but they pick the ones who have the best reasons. Once selected, they're trained and trained and trained some more, going up against any spell that anyone can think of that will murder another or influence them. They learn to shield them-selves, learn to pick up the subtle signs. Grant would have gone through a lot of the same training, but not to the same degree."

"And Lucas?" I asked.

"Lucas is just a mage with solid spirit magic. He teaches and when he's not teaching, he lives in the enclave teaching tai chi to the inhabitants," Win said. "He's powerful but I think your level of magic is greater than his and you have more range. It makes you both useful and dangerous. I'm not sure even Jeremy, who was chosen largely because of how much magic he has, could take you on if you had enforcer training."

"How did I get so much magic? I mean, I know it's by accepting myself but…"

"For two reasons. The first is how much we accept ourselves and how much pressure there is on us not to accept ourselves. Lauren, for instance, is incredibly powerful because of messages she was given as a child that she had to overcome. Contrast that to your neighbor Sandra, who is far less powerful because the thing she is most ashamed is far less stig-matized by the general public than your shame or Lauren's. And don't say your shame aloud to me," Win held up a hand. "Spirits listen, too. The other reason is just like everything else, it depends upon the potential you're born with."

Another reminder that whatever gave us our power could be used against us. I thought about Grant and the potential attraction, how it made me worry about how I looked, how I wished suddenly to be thinner. It wasn't that I didn't often want to look fashionably thin, if only to fit into a world not built for me, but I'd allowed that wish to color how I thought of myself. I'd felt my powers being drained.

"Grant did something…" I started.

Win held up a hand. "I saw that in your mind just now. It suggests that someone planted a seed even before he arrived on the island or else the moment he stepped off the ferry."

"But it was only Gerald and Lucas and maybe Jack…" I trailed off.

"We haven't found Gerald. Ian wasn't paying attention to him when Grant came in. He was focused on Grant. He is an attractive man. However, that doesn't mean that Gerald couldn't have been down at the dock or going for a walk at just the right time. The fog warns everyone the ferry is coming," Win said.

"Gerald is still missing," I murmured. I hadn't thought about him, hadn't worried about him. I wondered how Carl felt, given that they'd been a couple.

Win shook her head. "I suspect, as you do, that he didn't leave and that he's in the main cave or the cavern system, hiding out. He'll do what he can to protect the heart. Now, I need to teach you about magical faucets…"

We spent a few minutes with Win teaching me how to create that faucet. The image was stronger than the one before and I had a better understanding of what she wanted me to do, so that took less time than the protection spells. Win smiled and was pleased in no time.

She got up and started moving her rollator towards the main table. I stood and followed her.

I noted Randi and Xavier had already gone back to the table and Rose was sipping a margarita. Elena had used the trip to also bring us several bags of food. Snack foods and sodas, of course, but also more sandwiches and fresh vegetables and cut fruit. I noted some of my favorite scones in the basket.

My eyes widened and I looked at Ian.

"They won't be as good as mine. Mine are handmade and these are mostly magic," he said.

I smiled and chose one. I shouldn't have been hungry again, but I was. Even the small amount of magic I'd expended with Win made me feel as if I'd used more energy than I should have. That didn't bode well for later on.

Jeanine rubbed her fingers.

"So, we ought to get started. If we're doing this today, once we start, we only have six hours to finish, or until we run out of magic," she said quietly.

That put a knot in my stomach.

"We'll weaken the hold if we take care of Grant first," Jeremy said. "We can eat more after that, even if it means a trip to Derry's."

"Do you need me to watch during this?" Carl asked.

Jeremy shook his head.

"Then I'll get start ordering. Any preferences?"

"Pasta," Elena said. "And bread. Sweets. We'll need plenty of quick fuel if we're going to head down to change the heart after this."

Carl nodded. He gave all of us a long look before heading out. But he placed a hand on my shoulder. "Be careful," he said. "I was new once, too, and this is a lot."

With that warning he was gone.

Chapter Nineteen

It took only moments for a slightly sour, rotten smell to fill the room. Jeremy, Elena, and Jeanine held hands as tingling began in my arms. The three of them focused on pushing back the barrier so they could get closer to Grant, to attempt to drive out whatever dark influences the heart had sent out to captivate him.

I moved to sit between Win and Ian, facing the barrier, watching. Bernice and Xavier stood next to each other just behind the three enforcers and Randi stood a little off to the side, her eyes narrowed. She was doing her usual job as a watcher, which literally meant to watch.

Xavier was tense, waiting for something, though I could infer what was going on with him. Bernice was her usual self, standing straight, not moving. She could have been waiting for a bus for all she gave away.

Jeremy had his legs spread and leaned slightly forward as if waiting to meet an opponent who would try and run him down. Given the way magic worked, perhaps that's what it felt like to fight another mage, at least for him.

Elena had one leg back and one leg forward, but she too leaned forward as if pushing into a wind.

The area around the doors became clearer in my vision and I thought I felt the barrier drop. The library had gotten so quiet, I could hear everyone breathing. Someone near the door was breathing harder than before, as if they'd already run a marathon. It worried me because the conflict had barely started.

The stink got stronger, making me want to gag. I didn't know how I'd ever been able to eat in the library with that aroma floating around.

Win waved the smell away with her hand. Normally such a thing didn't work, but it did for her.

My arms tingled so hard I wasn't sure I could move them.

The magic pressed against me like a strong wind and my eyelids fluttered closed. In my mind's eye I saw Bernice and Xavier. The magic flowed past them and toward us like a brownish red sludge. I sensed a force from it, a need to swallow everyone, to destroy.

The three enforcers pushed it around, thinning it out, creating holes, but the magical sludge only sealed itself back up.

I noted that Win kept it away from us with hardly a second thought. Purple magic like a ribbon floated up behind me and I knew that was Rose working her own magic against the sludge.

My arms had gone beyond tingling and into pain. I hated being so sensitive to the magic. I wished my arms would toughen up against the sensation, rather like the soles of my feet against rocks if I went barefoot for a long time.

Sounds rushed around me, muffled, as if I were underwater. I saw Sharon punch through the purple wall and head towards me. I put up my protections, the ones that Win had taught me. I should have done so earlier.

I felt pressure on my chest as Sharon started to bang on the walls of protection. Lucas had said she was all brute force, and once again, he was right. While my barriers remained solid, I gasped for breath. I could take shallow breaths, but it took effort. My heart pounded as if I were doing a heavy workout.

Sweat tickled my neck.

Sharon, meanwhile, just kept probing for imperfections in my protection. She pressed against the barrier, almost as if she knew it made it harder for me to breathe.

I saw another spirit, a darker one. This one was just bone with traces of flesh hanging off. Sometimes spirits didn't look like themselves. Win would probably tell me it was because they'd forgotten what they'd appeared in life. Sharon still remembered, so she looked like herself, if a bit thinner and paler.

This other spirit had darkness surrounding it. The bones were ashy. Power emanated from the spirit as it beat at my protection spell. The walls threatened to crumble. I pushed back with everything I had.

Whoever this spirit was, he was strong and he was angry. I immediately thought of Damien. But Damien would probably look like himself. I felt, more than saw, traces of Damien's energy. This spirit had absorbed it.

While Sharon's pressure had ultimately been futile, this spirit had magic, which spirits didn't normally have, not in that way. They had their own powers, but not real magic. The angry spirit fought my protection spells magically. I responded by shoring them up with all the energy I could muster. The spirit used magic to drain my protection.

I needed help, but didn't know how to get it.

Opening my eyes, so at least I didn't see the creature

who was coming at me like a zombie in a horror movie, I saw that Ian and Win were also fighting. Win was looking less certain and less powerful. Her face was pale.

"I've got you," she whispered. "Close your eyes. It's the heart. You need to focus on keeping it away from you."

I closed my eyes and focused on keeping the spirit at bay. I imagined my walls as being thicker. I pictured myself in another room with other barriers. I couldn't make them all as strong as the outermost one, but because I moved myself deeper into a magical house, I had more space, which took the pressure off my chest.

Sharon screamed, a long, loud siren of anger. It hurt my ears. I resisted the impulse to cover them and hide from the sound. I folded my hands in my lap and my fingers grasped each other so hard that my knuckles throbbed.

I used that pain and that anger to fuel my power, strengthening my protection spells further.

Vaguely, beyond the creepy skeleton spirit that was supposed to be the heart, beyond Sharon, and even beyond Xavier and Bernice who appeared to fighting their way through swampy sludge, I saw Jeremy, Elena, and Jeanine walking through the magic. Jeanine seemed to have a device that vacuumed up the magic, lessening it. Jeremy pulled away at something that looked like cobwebs.

Elena had set protection spells around all of them and pushed against the magic that surrounded them from behind until Jeanine could pull it into the device.

Each person's magic was a vivid color in my mind's eye. I saw Rose's purple magic. Win's was a deep burgundy. Jeremy's gold. Elena had a soothing teal blue, and Jeanine had a darker, almost ominous navy blue around her, though it sparkled with silvery spots here and there.

I looked away from them, the colors hurting my eyes. As I did so I noticed a pinkish flow of magic coming from down the hall. It was shot through with black and reminded me of nothing so much as an artist's rendering of blood flowing down a hallway cloaked in shadows.

It wrapped talons of pink and black around Jeremy but he fought them off. He gestured with his hands a few times, almost as if he were cutting off the talons. Jeanine was right there, clearing away the magic, dulling the colors.

I could watch so long as I didn't look directly as the people doing magic. The colors quickly diffused and became a kaleidoscope behind my eyes.

Meanwhile, the creature that was after me turned and moved towards the three enforcers. Elena put up a wall. The teal glowed. I saw how she'd created the magical wall, thick and wide, and multi-dimensional. While the heart came at them directly, even when it pushed against them, Elena seemed more at ease with keeping it out than I did.

I attempted to create a wall not unlike hers, putting it around me, between me and Sharon. But I wasn't able to create such a thick, wide wall. Mine looked like a thin spider web rather than the thick, solidity of Elena's. I'd have to ask Win how to do that later on.

Over a sound like rushing water, I heard Ian groan.

My eyelids flew open. He looked pale and gray. I moved to touch him. He glanced at me, but shook his head.

Of course. He had magic from the island. I wondered if he were fighting with the spectral image of the heart for control of the island's magic.

Something pulled at me. My eyes fluttered closed again. Another pull and the spectral image disappeared. Elena's teal colors flared making the world look slightly teal. Then gold flashed brightly like the sun from behind a cloud.

I turned away slightly.

Sharon's spirit had been nearby. She vanished with the flare of gold.

The momentary flash of gold was so bright it hurt. I added something to my protection spell to protect me from bright lights.

It helped, but I still couldn't see anything beyond the colors. The gold blended with teal. I couldn't make out the figures of the enforcers at all.

I heard someone—a woman—cry out briefly. The cry stopped suddenly. A lump formed in my throat, as I worried she'd been hurt.

The colors disappeared. My arms ached from the after effects of all the magic. The pain quickly eased into my usual tingle.

I opened my eyes. Win held her hands out in front of her.

Ian sat straighter, breathing easier. Randi knelt between us and the enforcers. Bernice stood off to one side, head high. Xavier was on the other side. He looked a bit shrunken, but his hands were at his side, palms up.

I couldn't see magic with my eyes open, but I knew Xavier was using it, just as I knew Win continued to work her spells. I wasn't sure about Ian or Rose. The agony in my arms eased, but didn't completely go away.

Jeremy, Elena, and Jeanine walked slowly down the hallway.

I wanted to ask what had happened, why Randi was kneeling, but I didn't want to interrupt. Even if I had wanted to interrupt, the tingling danced down my arms again, enough to distract me from my question.

I closed my eyes, hoping the flare of teal and gold was gone. It was, though I could see the colors briefly from the hallway, where the enforcers had disappeared. Randi remained where she was. Bernice guarded the door, her magic silvery blue. As I watched, she created another barrier.

Rose's purple magic infused the silvery blue so that the barrier itself was gorgeous. Unfortunately, it kept me from seeing what was going on beyond it as well.

I looked down at where Randi should be, but I saw nothing when I looked at her. Worrying, I thought maybe she was dead. I opened my eyes, prepared to go to her. But she was breathing. She just wasn't doing magic. Perhaps that's why I hadn't noticed Bernice or Xavier when I'd watched the others. If they were doing magic, it was far more subtle.

Still, Randi appeared weak. I started to push myself up to assist her.

Ian put a hand on me, pushing me back. I glanced at him. He gave a single shake of his head. I shouldn't leave my place.

Hopefully, Randi would be okay. That she'd just stopped using her magic, which had been a pale yellow, nearly invisible against the gold flares Jeremy had, worried me. Something had happened.

My stomach growled, now that I wasn't fighting off Sharon or the heart. I continued to hold a protection spell around me because it seemed like the smart thing to do. I would need to eat after this. I hoped Carl was bringing plenty of food.

Magic flared around me, making my arms ache again.

Rose's purple joined with my protection spell and then with Win's deep burgundy magic.

I groaned as the pain in my arms reached down through my chest and into my core. I wanted to curl up and hold my stomach, to move away from the pain like a wounded animal, but there was nowhere to go.

I opened my eyes to see Gerald hurrying towards

Randi. She held up a hand, her pale yellow magic flaring, pushing against him. It wasn't nearly enough. Bernice turned, her magic already flashing, ready to incapacitate him

Gerald sent out a tendril of sickly, waxy-looking green that wrapped around Bernice's magic and sent it back at her. She was able to catch it, but it gave him time to grab Randi.

Randi was still wrapped in her own protection spells.

Gerald's arm sliced through them with ease.

I closed my eyes again and noticed the spectral creature that was the heart working with him. Randi didn't have the power to fend off the heart.

While I watched, her yellow protection spell faltered and Gerald dragged her away from the main door.

Chapter Twenty

"Stop." Ian's voice echoed through the library. It wasn't such a loud order as much as it was forceful. The reverberation of the command echoed through my body, making me want to pause what I was doing until Ian gave me further instructions. I pushed against the command, knowing Ian hadn't meant me.

I created a protection spell which I tried to wrap around Randi.

Gerald's power pushed it away as if it were air.

I knew I had done a good job and I knew my power was strong, but he made it seem like nothing. Of course, he was acting for the heart that had been blackened and hardened over centuries.

Win used her rollator to walk over to Gerald. I saw strands of her magic surrounding her. Ian's flashy magic surrounded her as well.

Win tried to grab Gerald, but he leaned out of the way. As he did so, he sent a bolt of magic towards her, though more slowly than I would have expected.

Despite that, I winced. Win rolled out of the way,

sprier than I would have expected of a woman with a rollator.

The magic dissipated against Win's magical shield.

Gerald attempted to turn and leave. His muscles strained in the attempt to go, but he couldn't move.

Ian's order had been directed at him. Gerald could protect himself from what he saw as threats, but he couldn't go anywhere.

He also couldn't grab Randi, though his arm remained inside the area that should have protected her.

Slowly, his muscles bulging here and there through his clothing, Gerald reached down around his back where I noted he had a gun lodged.

Sweat beaded on his forehead even as his fingers wrapped around the handle, grasping it. Knuckles white, arms shaking, he pulled it from his waistband.

With equal slowness, he raised the gun, aiming generally in Win's direction, as if he were going to shoot her.

I hurried toward him.

Win stood serenely in front of him. I knew her spells were strong, but there was always the possibility that the heart would weaken them enough that a bullet could go through. It wouldn't let something kill her, but she could be badly injured. At her age, I didn't know what that would mean.

"Holly! Stop!" Ian yelled. I looked back at him. He shook his head.

"He can defend himself against you," Ian said. "And I'm not sure the magic alone can save your life if you try and go up against him. The heart is letting him access the island's magic."

Sharon appeared, because, of course she did.

"Kill her!" Sharon shouted at Gerald.

No else reacted.

I remembered a few of the simple things Lucas had taught me. I could order a spirit to be gone, much the same way Ian had ordered Gerald to stop.

I drew in my magic. I felt the heat of my body rising up, the way I had learned the first day, when Sharon had shown me I had magic.

I used the magic, pushed it into the command I gave her, using my finger to point at her, "Sharon! Be. Gone. Spirit!"

The magic spilled out of me. I watched as Sharon, who looked as real as any person in the room was ripped to shreds by my magic. There wasn't any blood, of course, though her body was shredded like toilet paper before a cat's claws.

"Very nice," Win said. "I didn't see her, but she's gone. I could feel it. I think she's gone for good this time."

I didn't turn to her. I watched Gerald who was now glaring at me. He attempted to aim the gun at me but his arm strained merely to lift it.

Randi rose to her feet and chanted something quietly under her breath. I half closed my eyes, enough so that I could see her yellow magic encircling him. It looked to me as if he were being encased in ice, freezing him—perhaps literally—in place.

"He'll free himself in a few minutes," Randi said. She shook her head, like she was clearing it.

I glanced up. Xavier looked like he was pushing against a boulder. Bernice's hands were flying around at whatever magic they were dealing with in the hallway.

I heard a woman's voice gasp, loudly. My heart thudded. I'd been confident that the enforcers could work to free Grant Arwen. Jeremy's certainty had given me that confidence. But someone was clearly injured.

Randi turned. "That's Jeanine…" She shook her head and then glared at Gerald.

The freeze was already melting. Randi did another spell despite the fatigue that strained her muscles. The spell took shape slowly, nearly as slow as Gerald's movements as he fought against Ian's spell.

"I've got it," Rose said, quietly.

She wobbled around, raising her shaking hand. Gerald straightened, rather as if he were surprised. He didn't seem frozen any longer, but it was clear he couldn't move.

"That will hold at least until I prepare for the ceremony," Rose said.

"I'll kill you first…" Gerald managed. "The island will let me. The heart doesn't want you."

"The heart will get me, one way or another," Rose said. "If I die, I'll die here, and I'll be one of the spirits influencing it for good. I doubt I can change it, it's so tarnished, but I'll do what I can. If we succeed in our efforts, I'll be anchoring the enclave as the new heart."

Gerald growled, a low tone without words.

Rose tottered back to her chair, her head bobbing a bit. "I guess the margarita didn't keep me from working my magic."

Ian barked a half laugh, though he bit his lip looking down the hallway.

My arms abruptly stopped tingling again. Now they just ached as if someone had been grabbing them and holding me down for a long period of time.

Elena walked out, half carrying Jeanine. Jeremy didn't reappear.

I bit down on my lip, determined not to show any emotion. It wasn't as if we had a relationship. He'd gone to lunch with me while guarding me. He admired my magic.

While he'd been nice, it wasn't as if we could've had a relationship.

But that didn't matter in that moment. I had that hope. The idea that maybe, no matter how far-fetched, that we could have been something. And now he wasn't there.

Neither was Grant. I was not exactly a lucky girl in the objects of my lust. Not that day.

Bernice leaned over and put her hands on her knees. It was about as much emotion as I'd ever seen from her.

Jeanine's head lolled to the side. I saw her chest rising and falling, so she was alive, at least.

Xavier leaned against the door, trying to push himself inside, but not doing a good job.

Randi walked over and put a hand on his shoulder as both looked down the hall.

Elena settled Jeanine on the floor near the table. Ian bent over her. He raised his head to survey the food and drink we had. There was iced tea but nothing hot. He grabbed a bottle of the flavored iced tea. My arms tingled slightly. And then he held that up to Jeanine's mouth so she could drink.

"Thanks," Elena breathed quietly. "We all overdid it. At least if we were planning on replacing the heart."

Just then, Carl came in with more food. He paused, looking at Gerald who remained in the stasis in which he'd been placed. There was a hint of a glare from Carl, but when he noticed the people kneeling on the floor on the other side of the table, he hurried over with the bags.

Once those were set down, Carl turned back to Gerald. I could see he was torn, wanting to vent his anger, but knowing he needed to help. He took a single step towards the man that he'd had an on-again, off-again relationship with before stopping. His shoulders slumped. He shook his head.

"I can't believe..." his voice trailed off.

I grabbed a soda and went over to Randi, handing it to her, while Carl looked around, attempting to take in everything, to figure out what had happened.

"Jeremy?" Carl asked the question I hadn't been able to voice.

"*He's* fine," Elena said, the emphasis on the pronoun making it clear that no one else was.

"Where?" Carl gave her a soda as well and a bag with some chips. It helps when you've over done it to start with smaller foods. It forces you to eat more slowly rather than gulping down a pound of steak or something.

"Down the hallway. With Grant," Elena said. "Jeanine couldn't sever the connection completely. It would have killed him. It bounced back at her. Jeremy managed it with his usual lack of finesse. Grant is hanging on, barely. I don't know if he'll make it."

Ian glanced at Win.

"It's safe enough down there, now. You should be able to protect yourself against any residual," Win told him.

Ian hurried down the hallway, carrying some teas and food. He preferred to use his magic on teas and coffees rather than soda. He'd told me once recently that it was harder for him to work with the ingredients in soda, to pump them up, as he put it.

I went back to the table to sort through the food and drink Carl had brought.

"There's more in the golf cart," Carl said. "It's what took me so long. Derry's had to do some cooking." He leaned against a chair, head down, as if the little he'd done was more than he could bear. Given his connection to Gerald, perhaps it was.

"I'll go," Win said, pushing her rollator back.

"I can do it," I said.

Win shook her head. "It's not safe. You're too powerful for us if the island influences you. Stay here with Elena and the others. Don't go anywhere on your own, no matter what. I'm not sure it's even safe for you to use the bathroom alone right now."

I sighed. I hated standing around watching Win go out to get food while I brought small packages to Randi. I hoped I was bringing things she liked. However, she grabbed whatever I brought and wolfed it down. I took some food over to Bernice and Xavier as well. While both were hungry, neither was as ravenous as Randi. I wondered what she had been doing while the enforcers had worked. I had paid less attention to her magic, though with all the bright colors, hers had been easy to overlook.

Carl meanwhile, had sunk down into a chair and stared at Gerald, not speaking. His hands worked their way into fists and then eased, slowly, fingers opening one by one. He opened his mouth a few times to speak, but said nothing.

Win arrived back in the library with bags in the basket on front of her rollator. She pushed her way in, moving as quickly as she could.

"There's a storm brewing," she said. "It doesn't feel natural, but I bet it's so that the ferry can't get here in the morning. The heart is doing everything it can to try and delay."

Elena looked defeated. "Jeanine practically dies and it looks like Jeremy will still get his wish to push us through this on our own."

As I passed out food, I realized that the library smelled of French fries and garlic rather than the rotting stink of meat. Faint traces of the earlier aroma lingered in the back of my throat, but even so, I appreciated the change. I hoped that my taste buds wouldn't be flavoring my food with rot.

Elena and Ian mumbled at Jeanine. I sat with Win. Jeremy still didn't appear. Bernice came over, moving slowly, and got some more food. Xavier drank a soda and ate some fries by the door, watching the hall. Randi had tucked into a serving of pasta.

Carl sat behind us, his arms now crossed, staring at Gerald, still not speaking, a range of emotions crossing his face before falling back into his usual placid expression that had to cover a multitude of feelings. Gerald remained in a sort of stasis. His eyes roamed between us, but he was unable to move anything else. I wondered if his legs got tired from standing so still, or worse, if he had an itch somewhere that he couldn't scratch. Although, considering he was working on destroying the island, perhaps that itch would be a well-deserved mini-hell.

"I don't understand why someone would want to destroy the enclave," I said. "I get wanting power, but if the enclave is gone…"

Win shook her head. "Just because the heart goes bad doesn't mean the enclave will be destroyed. If someone who aligns with the dark vision comes in, they can sap some of that power. I used to think that because we had to delve into our own shame and deal with it, that we'd all be good people. Unfortunately, there are those who feed on disaster, and those who just don't like people. Maybe that's their shame. Maybe they get power from their dislike of others. The magic doesn't think in terms of right or wrong as humans do." The old woman shrugged.

I noticed she was eating quickly. She picked one of the desserts.

Randi was doing better, but Jeanine was still out.

Elena had refused to let her be taken to the clinic. She wanted to be with her.

"I need to be here to back up Jeremy if he gets into trouble," Elena said, a slight sneer in her voice. She was not happy about backing up Jeremy when her partner was down.

Ian continued to dribble fluids into Jeanine's mouth. Every few minutes I'd feel my arms tingle and knew he was working his magic. There had been some hot tea brought in as well and Ian was working with that, saving the hot liquid for Jeanine. The rest of us got the cold, bottled drinks.

I looked up at sounds coming from the hallway. Jeremy walked down the hall, supporting Grant Arwen over one shoulder. His eyes flicked to Gerald, who stood still in the middle of the room. Then he let Grant slump to the ground near the door.

"He's clear, but I want him off the island as soon as we can get someone here. I don't want to wait for the ferry."

Jeremy gave Xavier a pointed look, one that should have had subordinate hoping to do his bidding. No doubt Jeremy expected him to call someone.

I remembered that I'd been told back when I'd first arrived that there were mages who lived on the mainland who had boats. They could be called in when we needed something too big to fit on the ferry. They could be called in now, too.

Xavier got on the phone. Win sighed, shaking her head a little.

Rose leaned back and watched.

In a few minutes Xavier hung up his cell phone and shook his head.

"What?" Jeremy demanded. This arrogant, authoritarian person had been the enforcer I had seen on the island last month. He'd seemed softer this time, more caring, but I'd clearly allowed myself to be fooled. I couldn't believe I'd found him attractive. Not that I could blame for him his harshness, not just then.

"Storm coming in," Xavier said. "Waves are already plenty high and it's expected to get worse overnight. They aren't even sure the ferry will get through in the morning. It's not a natural storm, either. Nothing on the weather radar predicted this. It just appeared over the lake and the coastal areas."

Jeremy swore.

While no one else swore, and having heard what Win said about the storm, no one else was surprised, but I could see faces drop. More defeated than angry.

Jeremy walked over and grabbed a soda. I should have

given him one, but hadn't even thought. He chugged it down. The sugar helped his color though I noticed his hands shook slightly.

Rose passed him some fries.

He grabbed a handful and turned around. I felt a tingle on my arms. He was doing magic even as he took in what was happening.

"We need to segregate Grant somewhere. Who's left on the island?" he asked.

Ian closed his eyes. "David might be powerful enough to hold Grant and to avoid being influenced. He'd be my choice. Have him go to the B&B. It'll be safer there."

Jeremy nodded and pointed at Bernice to make that call, which she did. Then he stared at Gerald.

"We can put him in a cell at the station. Who's still around to keep watch?" Jeremy asked.

Ian closed his eyes. "The only one with good protection magic who probably has a clue what's going on is Gretchen. I'd pick Cassandra, but she's busy at the clinic with Dr. Mulrooney. We've had a number of people fall ill, probably to keep those two busy."

Nodding, Jeremy rubbed his chin.

"Who has power and knows Gretchen?" Elena asked.

"I'd have picked Lauren, but she's in the clinic," Ian said. "Holly could watch…"

Jeremy immediately shook his head.

"She'd be useful there," Win argued. "And she's good at protecting herself. Hell, she helped protect Randi when Gerald came in."

"She's too valuable to them. I want her with people strong enough to take her down the moment anything influences her," Jeremy argued. "Not Holly."

Take me down? I disliked the sound of that. I sniffed the air but no hint of rot followed Jeremy. He wasn't part of the problem. Just a problem for me. My emotions were ping pong balls bouncing between attraction and dislike.

"Then I'm not sure who," Ian snapped. "A lot of people left the island. And everyone else is busy doing something we need done. We have some of our best water magic folks out looking for Jack…"

Ian continued, but I was stunned. I had no idea people were looking for Jack. I hoped they found him. The fact that larger craft were being warned away from the water boded ill for him if he were still on the lake.

"And that doesn't even begin to scratch the surface," Ian finished. He put a hand on his hip and glared at Jeremy. Ian was back.

"How many people are still on the island?" Elena asked.

"Plenty," Ian said. "Too many to try and evacuate, if that's your next question. Most of them are like Gretchen. They live on the outer edges of the island and are probably already feeling the storm. I know Dirk and Bill left, but most of the others are staying with their animals, not the magical ones, but the livestock that give us our eggs and milk."

Long ago, I'd asked Ian how the island got its food and I remembered he mentioned a lot of farmers. Dirk and Bill, who I knew from the mornings I ate at the B&B, farmed. They'd no doubt left their livestock with someone else to watch. I didn't know how many other people had animals.

Gretchen didn't have animals, but she grew herbs and summer vegetables. She had a greenhouse, too, though she wasn't able to sustain the entire island with what she grew. It was mostly a supplemental thing. She enjoyed gardening, especially cultivating the herbs.

"But there must be more who have stronger powers," Jeremy pushed.

"Most of the people with the strongest powers were the ones who left," Ian said. "I think they felt what was coming the most clearly."

It made sense. I wondered why Gretchen had stayed, unless she felt it was her duty. David would have felt a duty to stay as well. He might run a clothing store on the island, but he'd been a minister in his former life. He'd gone through some stuff and had, as he put, lost his faith for a time and left the church. Still, he now held a non-denominational worship service on Sundays. I'd gone once and it was pleasant. He also ran a meditation group in the evenings, though sometimes Gretchen led meditation instead of him.

"Just admit we don't have the people to do everything you need us to do," Elena snapped.

Jeanine groaned just then, distracting both Elena and Ian. They moved to minster to her.

Jeremy looked frustrated.

"We can't re-dedicate the enclave if we don't have the five of us and I can't risk having Gerald running around, nor can I have Grant getting re-influenced."

David arrived, having been called by Xavier. David conferred with him and the two men went to get Grant. Carl watched, not moving, though I noted his muscles were tense, waiting to go if called.

"Why not Carl?" I whispered to Rose.

"I think they want him to help out with the transfer," Rose said. "And since Carl and Gerald were close, I suspect that Jeremy doesn't want him there in case he's got some loyalty to the man."

That made sense. Gerald was the reason Carl and I weren't together. Of course, we'd always been better as friends than dating partners. It was nice to be admired, but the physical attraction wasn't there on my side. Not like it was for Jeremy or Grant. Maybe I was too hyper-focused on what a guy looked like. Both of them were handsome, at least in my eyes. I sighed, trying to think if I knew of anyone with particularly strong magic that wasn't already sitting in the library.

Xavier came back in, looking harried and hungry. He went over to one of the tables to grab something more to eat.

"What about Katrina?" I asked. "I mean she always gets a flash of people's shame. Is that a major power?"

I didn't know her. Had sort of avoided her considering that I'd heard she could cause people's magic to falter. But I remembered Bernice telling me about her.

Ian nodded. "She's not traditionally powerful, but she's definitely got a different base of magic, which would make her harder to influence."

Jeremy glanced over at me with an expression of approval.

"Is she here?" he asked when he turned back to Ian.

"She is," Ian said.

The order to call her was given to no one in particular, but Xavier picked up his phone. Bernice continued eating. I picked at food, full from the stuff I'd already eaten. My body still felt empty. I had a feeling I'd be eating again as soon as I digested some of what I'd just had. Heavy magic could do that to a person. At least this time I didn't feel as if I'd over-extended myself.

Once calls were made, Jeremy sat down and ate. Now that Jeanine was sitting up, Elena grabbed more food and ate with her partner. Ian joined us at the table. He had food, but he wasn't as ravenous as the enforcers. He gave me a thin smile and a nod, as if he too approved that I'd remembered Katrina.

No one talked. Xavier and Bernice came back to the table to eat with us. There was no reason to guard the hallway now that Grant was out of the building.

"We should turn off the lights and lock up when we leave," Ian reminded us. "Lauren would have a fit if we didn't. If Reg were still here, so would he."

Bernice nodded. She nibbled at some bread, clearly full, but like me, wanting more.

"We need to get to the center of the island," Jeremy said. "Where the original heart was sacrificed. I think Ian and Holly know where it is. Right?"

Ian nodded, so I didn't have to. I did not want to have to go back down to the caverns again.

"We don't need to be inside the cavern," Win said quietly. "It can be done in the field. Of course, we'll get wet."

And as if she'd made a prediction, I heard rain lashing at the windows outside the library. The storm had arrived.

Chapter Twenty-Two

Somewhere around two hours later we were settled in the clinic. I had a bed, where I wasn't sleeping, in a shared room with Win. She snored softly. Our room was a standard hospital room, too plain with tile floors and pale walls that held only a board where notes could be written. Two chairs sat off to one side, but no one used them. Win had the bed nearest the door because there was a larger space between her and the bathroom where her rollator could be parked.

Before we got there, everyone had argued about what to do next. Jeremy had wanted to start re-dedicating the enclave as soon as people had eaten. Elena refused, saying she and Jeanine weren't up to it.

I had to side with Elena on that one. I hadn't used nearly as much magic, but I was already feeling vulnerable. Once Jeremy had finally acquiesced to the fact that most of us, and especially Jeanine, needed rest as well as food, they'd argued about where to sleep.

The B&B was the obvious choice, but Grant Arwen was there with David. Jeremy didn't like that. He worried, and according to Rose, rightly so, that Grant might still be susceptible to the current heart's influence. Staying and sleeping so close to him could be problematic. Ian had argued that the B&B was his and he felt safest there.

Jeremy won the argument about not going to the B&B, with Elena, Randi, and Bernice siding with him. No one else had an opinion, though Rose looked sympathetic to Ian.

We briefly considered camping out in the library, though Elena hadn't liked that. I couldn't say that anyone was thrilled with the idea, but once again, Jeremy worried about traces of negativity coming from the conference rooms.

The police station was out. Gretchen and Katrina were there, guarding Gerald. Nor was there any place to sleep since Gerald occupied the only cell. At least the library was carpeted.

Bernice suggested the clinic and no one had a good reason not to go there. Dr. Mulrooney, Cassandra, and Rebecca would probably all be there, and none of them had been influenced. Lauren, too, would be there, and I hoped to visit her. Everyone, even Lauren, who was awake and recovering, were all reasonably powerful mages, though not on par with the enforcers.

Getting to the clinic had been the next hurdle. The island didn't offer us enough umbrellas. The urn had appeared, but this was the first time that it hadn't refilled itself as someone took one.

Even if the urns had worked the way they usually did, Jeanine couldn't walk that far. Carl had used a golf cart to bring food from Derry's and it was finally decided that Rose would drive Jeanine to the clinic

The rest of us huddled under shared umbrellas. We could have waited to be ferried back and forth in the cart, but Jeremy was in a hurry to close up the library and lock it down. He was the last of us to get to the clinic. He'd looked like a drowned rat when he'd finally arrived.

Fortunately, there were showers attached to the rooms where he could warm up under the water. Dr. Mulrooney also had plenty of grab and go food for when she needed a boost, so we wouldn't go hungry. Xavier had called over to Derry's for more food and some unlucky worker would get to walk it over to the clinic. Fortunately, the worker was able to get an umbrella so our food wasn't soaked and neither was the worker.

The one good thing that came out of the move to the clinic was that Ian and I got to visit Lauren. I'd been surprised at how pale and gaunt she looked. Without makeup and her lovely clothing, Lauren's face looked far more androgynous than her usual feminine self.

If the white and blue gowns of the hospital made her look washed out, I had to admit that no one looked particularly good in one of those. The fact that her eyes looked deeper set than normal was probably due to fatigue and pain.

Lauren had been sleepy, but had thanked us for coming, curious about what was happening. She asked if we'd learned any more about the person who had been chosen as the original founding heart.

"If you can find something important to him, something he loved, like a child, that might help. It could ground him in who he was and make him less likely to fight you, or at least to not fight as hard," Lauren said quietly.

I suggested that to Win, who took the idea to Elena. She and Randi went back to the library to pick up some of the history books and bring them back. In theory they were reading them before falling asleep. Considering the snores coming from the room that Elena and Jeanine shared next door, I suspected that there wasn't much reading going on.

Pushing my pillow around, I tried to get comfortable. The clinic smelled of too much bleach and too many French fries. Only on Jewel could you end up with French fries in the hospital. Dr. Mulrooney knew better than anyone that the best way to help someone who'd overused their magic was to get them to eat plenty of high calorie foods.

The main sounds in the quiet building were snores, though sometimes I heard someone walk up and down the hallway. Having spent more time than I'd like to admit in the hospital over the last six months, I was fairly familiar with the sounds, so I knew the walker was Dr. Mulrooney.

Sighing, I forced my eyelids to close, certain that even though I was tired, my too-active mind wouldn't let me sleep. But, as it happened, I drifted off almost immediately.

I couldn't say how long I slept before I started to dream. Peony, my calico cat sat on the sofa in my home. She looked up at me and washed a paw.

"It's about time," she said.

"What?" I asked, wondering what I was late for. I had fed the cats that morning. They were probably hungry as they normally got food twice a day, but in my dream I wasn't sure how long it had been. "Can't you get your own food?"

"Of course I can," Peony said. "But I've been waiting for you to consult me. I know things."

"About the island?" I asked.

"About what you call the heart," Peony said. "I might be a magical construct, living and breathing like a cat, but I am so much more. We are founts of information." I knew Peony meant all the magical animals on the island, which meant most of them.

"But I've asked you things before and you don't answer," I said.

"Those were things you could discover on your own when you needed to. Didn't Tulip give you information when you wouldn't have found it otherwise?" Peony argued. She stood up, stretching. My beige sofa blended into the background.

Even so, as I walked towards it to sit, it came into focus. I settled on the sofa, studying my cat. I was obviously dreaming. My house had wood floors and while this room resembled my living room, this one had rugs that were not to my taste. They all looked rather like they had calico cat markings. The walls were a darker beige than the colors that were naturally there. The doors were painted blue, like large Siamese cat eyes. Both my cats were clearly involved in decorating this dream house.

If I were tempted to think I was awake, the lack of sounds would have kept me from falling into that belief. The refrigerator and HVAC were both silent. Like another person breathing, or snoring—and just then I thought heard echoes of Win's soft snores—my house had normal sounds. This one sounded dead. Empty, despite Peony's appearance. I stirred and the dream faded, but I pushed myself back into my home, visualizing myself on the sofa with the calico cat.

"Foolish," Peony said. "You almost woke yourself up. You knew you were dreaming…"

She washed her side, her tongue going quickly and deeply into her orange splotches of fur, pulling it aside from the white and pushing it over a black patch, the colors now damp from her saliva.

I waited, sitting on my sofa, which was darkening to black, as if the whole dream was becoming Peony colored.

"I am the one running this dream," Peony said. "The

new man, the one you met this morning. He's not clear. The others know some, but don't know that the influenced parts of him are waiting to strike. He'll attack David when you start the re-dedication ceremony."

"I need to tell someone," I said, turning to stand, wondering how to wake myself. It had been easy a moment ago.

"Not yet," Peony ordered.

I turned back to her.

"You banished Sharon earlier. Damien has gone, too. But…there are other restless spirits on the island. Some are helpful and love the enclave. Others remember only the worst of their lives. They aren't all spirits any longer. Some are shades without much thought—what is left is the energy of their lives. They are the main influences of the heart, now, that is not much more than a shade itself," Peony explained.

I nodded, glad to know that Sharon was gone.

"However, *you* can be influenced by those shades. The emotions will not be yours, but you will feel the things that they feel. The man you met in your office recently was attractive to them. That passed through you. You thought it was your own attraction, but it was theirs."

I wanted to ask about Jeremy.

"The enforcer is not attractive to them. They don't like him. He's arrogant and powerful and while that can be a dangerous combination, he doesn't care about his power so much as he cares about setting things right," Peony said reading my mind. Not a surprise considering she was in my dream. "He's rather particular about that."

"He is not easily influenced and because of that the heart will go after the others first, to push them not to do the ceremony, to find reasons to delay. The longer the delay, the greater the chance the ceremony never takes place. Already, a particularly formidable shade is worming its way into Jeanine. She fights it, of course, and for now she's winning. However, it's not gone and it *will* try again. She'll be weaker from this fight. When Jeanine finally loses her battle, Elena will fall because she trusts Jeanine. She'll refuse to see the changes."

"Are you certain?" I asked.

"Of course," Peony said, pausing in her washing, a paw half raised. Her large eyes stared into me.

"Warn them about the delays. It doesn't matter about David. He won't die. The magic won't let him no matter what the heart seeks. We are already pulling away from the heart. We would be further from it if the ceremony had been begun, but we cannot be joined to another without permission," Peony warned. "If we are forced to sever the tie before the heart is replaced, the enclave will be destroyed. And as you know, there is no island here in this lake."

I understood what the cat was saying.

"I will protect you as much as I can, as will all the constructs," Peony said. "But we are only magic. Without the heart, there is only so much we can do. You must guide us. Rose must take over guiding as much as she can even before the ceremony. It will increase your power."

Peony disappeared and I was running along the coast of the island, the cliffs that were low to the water, now towering above me as if I were in some movie about ancient Scotland. Waves crashed along the beach, attempting to reach me, to drag me under, the water deep and black. I knew there were horrors beyond imagining in those depths.

I pushed myself to run faster. I couldn't let the waters grab me. Even if it was a dream, the magic had reached me as I slept. I had no idea what else might find me.

I had to wake up. I had to climb the dream cliff. I found a place with handholds. I started up it, grabbing one and then another.

Even in my dream my hands cramped and spasmed, threatening to let go of the stones as I climbed. I could hardly breathe.

Again and again, I told myself to wake up.

Something grabbed my shoulder. I was certain it was a monster, but as I turned, I opened my eyes and found myself in the clinic bed, Win leaning over me, grasping the side of the bed, shaking me gently.

"That must have been some dream," she said.

I told her what I could remember, which, fortunately, seemed to be most of it.

"Then I think we need to start waking people," she said. "It's early but we've had some rest. Jeremy, no doubt, will thank us."

Win was dressed in one of the clinic gowns, which flowed like a Victorian nightgown, the place having decided the clinical blue and white gowns that people normally wore in a hospital were inappropriate for us. I had one of the Victorian gowns, too, one that fit every bit as well as what David would make for me.

She pushed herself over to her rollator and glanced at her clothing. "I'll go inform people. You get dressed. We're probably going to have a chat downstairs in the reception area. I'm sure there will be some who argue."

I rolled myself out of the bed, yawning. I still felt tired. But I also felt the wired sensation of being prepared to do something I didn't really want to do. Even if Win had recommended I sleep some more, I couldn't have done it.

Chapter Twenty-Three

Unsurprisingly, everyone argued. We sat in the reception area, a room I'd not spent much time in before, usually being taken into the clinic for my own good or passing through quickly to visit a patient.

I arrived first, having woken first and dressed quickly, so I had a chance to take the room in while people arrived in various states of dress and fatigue. Like the rest of the clinic's interior, the reception area had white and cream tile floors. Instead of beige, the walls were painted a pale teal. The chairs had pale oak frames and darker teal upholstered seats and backs. The arms were the same pale oak. I noticed that there weren't any armless chairs, but the one I planned to squish into widened to accommodate me. It wasn't quite as smooth as other places on the island. I actually felt the change in the chair, making me feel as if my body had gotten so large that it pushed the wooden arms apart to make room.

A silver urn of coffee sat in the corner. I made sure to get some, filling my plain cream colored mug. I sat back in my adjusted chair, glancing at the single picture on the wall. It was of the black stallion that lived towards the center of the island. Ian had told me the horse was the embodiment of the heart of the island. I wondered if that meant it was the embodiment of the heart or the magic, considering those things seemed to be separate.

I sipped the perfectly warmed coffee, tasting the bitterness on my tongue, hoping that it would perk me up as it flowed down my throat. I breathed in the fumes as I swallowed. The coffee urn was a popular place as everyone who came down immediately gravitated there before sitting.

Win was the last to arrive. She was dressed in the same clothing she'd worn in the library, a purple outfit far bolder than Ian's usual black jeans and plaid vests. He was back to his usual black jeans and this time had a black vest over a plain white shirt. He might have been going to a funeral, and, in a way, he was. Lauren had come down, dressed in a plainer outfit than usual, a sheath dress that fell to her knees and a fluffy pair of slippers in peach with little pig faces. When she'd turned to settle on a chair, I noticed that the slippers even had little curly tails on the heels.

Bernice looked as if she was ready to work, putting the rest of us, yawning and half-awake, to shame. I held my coffee in front of me, wishing I had Ian's magic to give it a bigger punch.

Dr. Mulrooney joined us for a moment, looking around at all of us. She looked tired as well. Her eyes narrowed when they landed on Lauren, but she said nothing to her about it in front of all of us.

"The coffee urn never empties," she said. "And no, I can't set you all up with IVs to the caffeine."

That drew a few chuckles.

"We need more rest," Elena persisted. "Now that we

know that Jeanine can fight off the influence, we can take longer to rest…"

Xavier shook his head. Jeremy was still sipping coffee. He seemed content to sit back and let our Chief of Police take the brunt of Elena's ire. Carl sat up, looking thunderous. It was unlike him, but no doubt after learning what had happened with Gerald, he was ready for a fight.

"We have to do it now. The cats don't often come in dreams…"

"Something I'm aware of, but they also feed off their owner's fears." Elena gave me a long glare as if I were the cause of all of this. I'd not tried to make the cat say anything. It had come to me. Said things to me.

"Holly is not given to being overly dramatic," Bernice said. "If anything, she's able to downplay her emotions. In her place, I'd have run to another enclave after Damien was taken away. Or else run from all enclaves as fast as possible."

It wasn't that the idea of running away hadn't crossed my mind. I just didn't see how I could create wealth without a job, which I badly needed. So I'd stayed. Not that I was going to share that now. Particularly not when I appreciated the show of support from Bernice, of all people.

"I also think Holly is correct," Win said. "I can feel the enclave pulling at itself, the magic on one side, the heart on the other. We don't have much time."

"None of us are at our full powers," Jeanine said. "Nor do we have all the enforcers we really need for this."

A gust of wind hit the side of the building, reminding us that we weren't likely to get reinforcements any time soon. Rain splattered against the glass so hard I thought it might break. I calmed myself, trying to be that not-overly dramatic person Bernice claimed I was. It was a good thing she couldn't read minds like Win.

"I'm ready," Jeremy said. "We could all use a big breakfast and then we should go. Has anyone called David to warn him about Grant?"

Xavier nodded. "He's prepared. He called in Jonas Withers to help."

Ian nodded, his face lighting up. "That should be fun."

Elena looked over at him. "Who is Jonas?"

"He's an old guy who lives in a shack on the far side of the island," Lauren said. "He's nearly deaf and probably the one person who is genuinely outright mean for no reason other than he can be. He's got a decent store of magic, though he's not what most people consider particularly strong. On the other hand, he's enough of a cynic that he's not likely to be influenced."

"You're saying he's not a bad guy, despite being a curmudgeon?" Jeremy asked, a half-smile curving his lips.

"Exactly!" Lauren said, laughing. I envied her ease at talking to Jeremy. He nodded and hid his smile.

Bernice looked skeptical but she kept her thoughts to herself. Xavier seemed pleased enough, just as Lauren was. I hadn't had the pleasure, if that's what it was, of meeting Jonas. He'd never been in to have the accounting office do his taxes.

"Has anyone heard if they've found Jack?" I asked.

"An enforcer out of Milwaukee picked him up just before the storm got really bad. They had a heck of a time getting in," Jeanine said. "I found a text on my phone from last night."

"We still have outside connections," Elena said. "It's not gone that far. We could send out some mages with good water magic to get a boat here…"

Jeremy was already shaking his head.

"A regular mage can't stand up to an enclave," he said. "They'd get halfway out and the boat would sink. They were lucky to get to Jack before he was killed."

He looked back down into his coffee mug as if it would have an answer or a way of persuading everyone. Then he made a slight face. He looked up to find me watching and gave me a small smile. My face heated and I looked away only to meet Ian's knowing smile, which was exactly what I didn't need.

"We need to do it now," Win said. "I'm tired, too. I can feel how tired everyone is, but I believe the magic. I don't think it was Holly's fears playing out through the cat. The enclave is trying to pull itself apart already. It will only get worse. I, personally, have no desire to be here if the enclave decides to dissolve itself."

The clinic began to shake, almost as if the land were agreeing with Win. Elena's face paled. Jeanine looked as if she might be ill.

Jeremy stood up as soon as it had stopped. "That's it…"

"Not before breakfast," Randi said. "We might have to do this, but we absolutely need to have fuel. I know I'm still running on empty. I'll be pushing myself. Ian was overworked yesterday, not to mention Jeanine had to be revived. Ideally, she should have at least a week of rest…"

Jeremy shook his head.

"Breakfast is smart," Win said. "We need to hurry, but we shouldn't be stupid."

"Derry's then," Jeremy said. "Let's get going. Jeanine, Win, and Rose can ride in the golf cart. The rest of us walk. We need to get there quickly."

He made eye contact with each of us. Ian sashayed up to take my arm, pulling me aside to hold me back. I knew he was going to ask about the look that I'd given Jeremy. I really didn't want to deal with his questions, but I didn't have a choice.

Ian let the others get ahead of us so we could talk. He held the umbrella and made sure I didn't get my hands on one so I had to stay with him or go out and get soaked.

"Tell me about Jeremy..." he said.

"Nothing to tell." My face heated.

"I think there's something. Did something happen while I was laid up in the hospital?"

I shook my head. "Nothing really. It just seems like lately I'm attracted to everyone." I tried to laugh it off.

Ian gave me a side-eye look. "Honey, that blush tells me things. You like him. And I have to admit he has a certain charisma."

"He's kind of a jerk," I said. "He's the one pushing us."

"I like confidence," Ian replied smiling. "Besides, it wouldn't be a forever thing. He's an enforcer traveling around. But it could be great fun as you both recover from re-dedicating the enclave."

"Hopefully I won't have too much recovering to do," I said.

Ian sighed and didn't look me in the eye.

"What do you know?" I hissed at him. We were passing the police station and about to turn the corner to Derry's. The rain lashed at us and if the umbrellas were non-magical we'd have been soaked despite them. But Jewel had decided to work with us and the umbrellas kept water off us even if it didn't fall straight down. It was like walking in your own tiny little phone booth or something.

"Win said it's supposed to be the hardest thing an Innkeeper has to do when you hold the enclave together. She'll back me up because I haven't had to test the limits of my power since re-connecting with the enclave. But the others, they have to sever the connection to the old heart and help Rose attach as the new one. It takes time and it's supposed to be exhausting. I have a feeling we're going to need your abilities."

"That I can do," I said. "I just hope I don't have to try and fight anything. I was able to see magic, not just feel it crawling around on my arms, during this last fight. Do you think I'm getting more powerful or just learning to use what I have?"

"I think you're learning," Ian said. "If Win is right, I'm not sure you can get more powerful. You know it's not just about how much shame you have. It's also some innate ability. It's not supposed to be advertised because the U council decided they didn't want hierarchies as to who was more powerful than whom, you know?"

I nodded.

"I think you've been working on tapping most of your full powers nearly the whole time you've been here. And you have a lot of power."

"And you?" I asked.

Ian smiled. "I'm the Innkeeper. I have access to the enclave's power. At least usually. Right now, it feels like being married to someone who turns your stomach. It's like I found out my husband kills baby bunnies or something horrible."

I made a face at him.

"Yeah, I'm ready to be out, too. But first we must eat!"

Ian stood back to allow me to enter Derry's first. The day was still a dark gray, pink striations of sunlight only barely peeking through clouds. The street had been silent, though that wasn't much of a surprise given the early hour and that half the enclave had already fled. It was still just a bit after six. I didn't know Derry's was open that early.

Perhaps the restaurant worked not unlike the B&B, accommodating the needs of the people of Jewel.

I noticed the elevator next to the stairs, which I didn't usually see. Win and Jeanine were inside. Rose stepped on the lowest step and disappeared from view.

I followed.

Only instead of the usual restaurant, I was transported to a cave-like place that didn't look very welcoming. My heart thudded wondering what had happened now.

Chapter Twenty-Four

A hand touched mine. I looked over. Ian had appeared next to me. The cave was dark enough that it was hard to make out anything other than the uneven walls and a stalagmite near where the podium for the restaurant would stand.

Listening, I heard voices, though they were muffled. And I smelled food among the dank, rocky smell of the place.

"I believe this might be the Hard Rock Café," Ian joked.

"We aren't in the middle of the island?" I asked, thinking this reminded me of the caves I had walked through when I'd been hiding from Damien.

"Nope. This is Derry's. Just a little different from what we're used to. I expect the heart is trying to scare us, or at least you, given that you've been down in the caverns more than most of us," Ian said.

"You're sure?" I hated this. I couldn't see people because it was so dark.

Ian conjured a small light and led me forward. The

cavern opened to a seating area. The others were already there, though I wasn't sure how Win had managed with her rollator across the uneven floor.

Small lights glowed around the room and the table had a large candle.

"Will they be able to cook with the cave look?" I asked. I wasn't that hungry, but knew how important food was. I wasn't in the mood for more sandwiches or cold cereal. Although the scones I loved were wonderful, I couldn't exactly exist just on them, though I might want to.

"The kitchen never changes," Ian said. "Just the public rooms."

Great. The table was large and rectangular. I grabbed a chair near Win who was at the head of the table with her rollator nearby.

"We're not normally open this early," Mindy said, looking a bit harried. Her hair wasn't combed as neatly as normal and she looked a bit uncomfortable with the cave atmosphere. "And Gerald hasn't shown up yet. I got a message to be here..."

I suppose that the island had somehow contacted her and let her know. Probably the same for the cooks. It hadn't, however, let her know what was going on with Gerald.

"I'm glad you got my message," Bernice said.

So perhaps it wasn't the island, but merely Bernice being her usual efficient self. I noticed she didn't share that Gerald wasn't likely coming back to Derry's.

Mindy nodded. "I called in the cooks and they're already making eggs and waffles. There's going to be sausage and bacon, too. Anyone want oatmeal? They didn't start any but it doesn't take long...."

A few people shrugged and others shook their head. No one nodded at the oatmeal.

"Drinks?" Mindy asked.

We ordered, most of us asking for coffee, some adding in fruit juices. When she came back, Mindy had carafes of orange juice and apple juice and smaller containers of cranberry juice and grapefruit juice on a large serving cart that bumped its way across the rocky floor. A large coffee urn was centered on it and she served coffee from there. A smaller urn held hot water for tea, of which there was a variety of choices in a wooden box that she placed so it was easily accessible.

If the cave hadn't been a bit cooler than the usual temperature in Derry's, this could have been a fun and unusual outing. Unfortunately, every light breeze that lifted the hairs on the back of my neck made me shudder. Every single imperfection on the walls reminded me of why we were there and why I didn't want to be there.

The food didn't take long and was served family style on large platters. There was plenty. I noticed that Randi and Jeanine ate quickly and voraciously. They both needed it. Everyone else wasn't far behind, although I was one of the lighter eaters, not having used as much magic as the others. I was hungry, but it was closer to an ordinary hunger than that of a mage who had overused her magic.

Ian pressed me to eat more, and barring that, to at least drink more orange juice.

"You'll need it later," he promised.

"If I drink too much I'll have to try and create a bathroom outside which is not my strong point," I said.

"You'll be fine." He chowed down on some toast, having eaten two fried eggs and a large pile of scrambled eggs, as well as a several sausages and a pile of bacon. All that came after the waffle he'd inhaled. Ian was definitely not quite himself. He'd either used more magic yesterday evening than I'd thought, or he was still recovering from having had to reconnect to the island. I suspected the latter.

I drank a little more orange juice, but I was full and wanted nothing more. Everyone else continued with their breakfasts.

I realized that I couldn't hear the rain outside. Normally in Derry's, I could. I mean I had no idea exactly where the building was, but usually there were windows that looked out over the street and towards the lake. Wind might whip around the eaves or rain might lash windows the way it would for a normal building up that high.

Today, it was as silent as if we were actually in a cave deep under the island. It made me wonder if Derry's moved around and we were just teleported to the exact spot or if the lack of sound was just because the magic assumed you wouldn't hear anything in a cave.

Lauren sat a few places down from me and she had also finished her breakfast. No one else appeared to have noticed that she'd joined us.

She met my eyes and gave a tight-lipped smile. I nodded back. Lauren pulled out a phone and started reading on it. I wondered if she'd found a way to research Ambrose Marchand. It wasn't impossible to find information on the enclaves online. You just had to know the right combination of words. And, I suspected, you needed to have magic to find certain things. Not that you needed to put a spell on stuff. Somehow the magic knew who had it and who didn't.

I pulled out my own phone to do a search, but I got no internet access. When I closed that out, I saw that I didn't have a phone connection either. Looking up, I noted that Lauren had put her phone away, looking troubled.

"What is it?" Ian asked. He was picking at another

rasher of bacon. As far as I could tell, he'd eaten the better part of a pig.

"Phones are down," I said quietly.

He closed his eyes, and my arms tingled.

"The storm is worse. I bet there are outages all around the lake."

Jeremy looked up. "We'll have to set up some sort of shelter out there."

"I can handle that," Lauren said. "I want to be there. To observe, of course. That's part of my job as librarian."

Jeremy nodded. "Holly can be your second. Both of you can lend power when and if we need it. The shelter is important, but not as important as the re-dedication."

"Did anyone find anything else out about the original heart?" Lauren asked. "I found a few tidbits, but nothing that seemed important."

"I fell asleep," Elena said.

Jeanine nodded. I knew she'd fallen asleep because of the snoring I'd heard.

"I know he wasn't married," Lauren said, "but was said to have loved a woman who died in a fire before he found his powers. He never really connected to anyone after her death other than just a general sort of friendly connection."

"He had to have been a good guy to have been chosen," Win said. "We've always had good instincts. Nor would the magic have accepted someone who wasn't decent."

"It sounds like it," Lauren said. "Helpful. Kind. Considerate, but not someone easy to know. I got the impression that he might have been mourning the love of his life for as long as he lived."

"Maybe we can use that," Elena said slowly. "I mean, we can try."

Jeremy said nothing.

"Are we finished eating?" Bernice asked, her hands ready to boost her out of her chair.

Nods all around.

She stood and the rest of us followed. I swallowed the lump of anxiety that had lodged in my throat. Everything felt so precarious. I was not looking forward to the next several hours.

Chapter Twenty-Five

There were enough umbrellas in the urn this time, but that wasn't much of a comfort. The rain poured, as hard as I'd ever seen. I'd heard about rain in sheets, but this seemed to be taking that metaphor literally. It cascaded into the little room at the bottom of the stairs as we filed out.

Jeanine, Rose, and Win got into the golf cart. By the time they managed that, they were all incredibly wet, having needed to walk around the cart and then maneuver the umbrellas around. The rest of us did what we could to keep them from being soaked through. I worried about how their damp clothes would affect their working.

Lauren had walked ahead with Elena. She'd be putting up the shelter. I hoped that she worked her magic quickly.

The rest of us didn't talk much. The drumming of the rain against the ground was too loud to make it easy to talk, which left all of us alone with our thoughts inside our little umbrella cocoons. Jeremy walked near me. Ian had given me a quick wink before scooting ahead to walk with Bernice.

It didn't really matter as no one was talking to anyone.

I wouldn't have known what to say even if I thought someone could hear me. I am typically not at a loss for words in a social situation. I mean, I'm not a huge talker but small talk is easy enough after years of being part of a large company where I was married to the owner's son.

Now, I worried about what was going to happen. I didn't want to show it, lest my fears distract someone from their jobs. Plus, with Ian's suggestive looks and glances, I felt like an awkward pre-teen with her first crush. I was really going to throttle him when this was over. Another reason to hope for our success—I could kill Ian, or at least threaten to.

Puddles formed in low spots so I picked my path carefully. Rose drove the golf cart slowly around us hoping to minimize the wash from the wheels, though the umbrellas kept most that water off of us as well. The only thing that it didn't help was if you stepped in one of the puddles that were growing from puddle ponds to puddle oceans.

When we reached the path that led to the field above the center of the island, the grass was soaked and the ground a muddy mess. Rose sped up as she reached the path, no doubt worried about getting stuck in the thick mud.

It wasn't a short walk and it was made longer by the harsh weather. The air wasn't particularly cool, but even though I was covered by an umbrella that kept the rain out, my clothes felt damp. I shuddered at how the women in the cart must feel after having gotten wet.

When we finally moved past the bushes that lined the path, we saw Lauren, Rose, Elena, and Jeanine, huddled under the large open-air, roofed building that Lauren had created. The floor was dry, hard-packed dirt. I wondered how she'd accomplished that. Large rollers lined the edges of the eaves of the roof. Once we were all inside, Lauren would be able to unroll those, closing the space against the rain.

It wasn't perfect, but it was better than I could have done. I'd have been lucky to manage a stepping stone. Earth magic was definitely not one of my fortes, though others with more earth magic could utilize what I had and channel it into their own magics. I had asked Bernice how that worked once and she'd given a complicated answer that I didn't quite understand.

When we'd gathered inside, the sides were lowered, protecting us from the rain. The island produced an urn where we deposited our umbrellas. It hadn't appeared until the flaps went down, suggesting that walls were required before the urns appeared.

Lauren made a low magical bed for Rose to lie down on.

Rose wobbled slowly there. She bobbed her head at each of us as she did so, though after the first person it was hard to know if it was directed at a particular person or if she just couldn't stop the movement. No one spoke. If anyone had had last words to say to her they must have said them last night. Xavier's eyes looked a bit moist, but he didn't cry. Carl reached out and held one of her hands in both of his, but just for a moment.

Rose settled in.

"I accept this duty freely. I have volunteered my heart to be the next heart of the enclave. I have not been pressured to do so. I will fulfill my part of the ceremony when the time comes. I speak the truth."

My arms tingled gently. Perhaps Rose had done a small spell to prove she wasn't being coerced.

Bernice, Randi, Elena, Jeanine, and Jeremy stood around Rose in a circle. Win and Ian held hands a bit behind on one side.

Xavier took his place to one side of me and Lauren. Carl stood on the other side, alert and waiting.

The tingling in my arms told me someone was doing magic. For some reason I believed it had come from Carl. Perhaps, as a watcher, he needed to magically record the ceremony.

The land rumbled.

I stumbled to the side.

I noticed Ian hanging on to one of the poles. Win's rollator had moved slightly, but she hadn't fallen. When he righted himself, Ian moved to stand beside her again.

Jeremy nodded at the circle.

The slight tingling in my arms became a deep, painful ache that I always felt when lots of magic was being done. Ian closed his eyes, his mouth clamped shut. Win looked down at the ground, nodding now and then.

"It's a go," she whispered.

Then, the magic really started.

I closed my eyes against the ache in my arms. I wished for a chair, because the ache was so deep and painful it radiated throughout my entire body.

Like before, I saw the spells behind my eyelids. Ian held something heavy, like a huge rock. He cradled it as if it were a baby. I wondered if the image was my own imaginative image of the enclave or if it were Ian's.

Win had a hand on him to help him steady his burden. The colors of their magic mingled, creating a beautiful collage. I wished I had the artistic ability to paint with those colors. I'd keep such a painting in my house.

Shadows moved around the tent, swaying in the breeze. A heavy wind attempted to fling the tent away. Though the gusts whistled and tore at the fabric, Lauren's magic held. I wondered how hard she was working to keep us dry.

One of the shadows approached me and stared. The shadow became a skull, all grinning teeth and hollow eyes.

While my heart pounded, I'd seen images of the dead before. I stood my ground, erecting a protection spell of the sort Win had taught me.

"I can break through that spell," the skull whispered, pounding at my barrier with an axe, though no arms held it.

I drew magic from deep within, attempting to force the heart away, but it wasn't enough. It was like pitting cardboard against the axe.

"I am still the enclave," the heart whispered. "I don't want to be destroyed. Not before I've had my revenge against the failed promises of those who put me through that ceremony. She will learn. She will learn that it's not right. That it's dark and horrible, that eternity eats away your soul, and what time doesn't destroy, the magic takes. Always   pressing.   Interfering.   Insisting.   Forcing. Imprisoning!"

I shuddered at the words.

I took a step back, but the skull remained in front of me, so close I would have felt it's breath, if it had any.

My head pounded, which usually meant something was attempting to possess me. I wouldn't let it happen.

I heard chanting and focused on reciting words I could barely hear. I spoke them softly, not so loud that I became part of the chants or the ceremony, but just enough to focus my mind on our purpose, on what we had to accomplish. We had to sever the connection this creature had to the enclave.

The creature rushed me, claws out.

I built another shield. In my mind's eye I pictured a steel shield like a Roman warrior might carry. Even using magic to create it, the shield weighed heavy on my arm, as if I weren't strong enough to carry it. But I was a big girl and used to pushing myself.

My imagination created a Roman coliseum. The ground was hard dirt, just like the dirt I stood on. Instead of cloth, white stone walls surrounded me in an oval, above which I noted seats. Most were empty. Ian and Win sat together, watching. Ian waved his hands to cheer me on.

Near a doorway, stood Xavier impassively watching, arms crossed over his bare chest. He wore only a sort of toga skirt with long silvery sandals that laced up to his knees. He didn't appear to notice either me or the creature in the coliseum's arena.

The creature changed into a full skeleton, with bones so large and broad that it looked only vaguely human. It created a sword and rushed at me before I understood what was happening.

I raised my shield again, but the crash of the heavy sword pushed me backwards a few steps.

I wanted a sword as well. My right hand immediately held a blade. Mine was shorter than the creature's, but was light enough for me to lift it and attempt to fight. Not that I'd ever been in a sword fight.

I parried as best I could, attempting to score a hit against the thing. Sometimes the creature faded in and out, but the coliseum remained around me. I backed towards the door, hoping that if I got beyond it, a gate would fall, sealing the creature in the arena.

The place smelled metallic and ripe. Deep down, I knew this imaginary world was conjuring up the stink of dead bodies that might have fallen there before me, of gladiators who actually knew how to fight with a sword.

The creature rushed me and cut my arm. Blood swirled on the ground. My arm stung.

Only then did I realize I didn't feel the tingles that I normally felt when magic swirled around.

Fear raced through me as I wondered where I was. My heart thudded harder. It had been one thing to fight, thinking this was some odd imaginary image of the fight I was having against the enclave itself, but it was another to think that perhaps I wasn't exactly in my body.

The creature faced me and laughed.

"But I am!" It cried.

I rushed at it, shield held high. I used my sword to slash at it, creating a cut on its torso. Blood flowed from it even more freely than from my arm, though it had no flesh to bleed. I backed away, pleased with myself, if confused about how this imaginary world worked.

The thing rushed me, hacking at my face.

I brought up both shield and sword and attempted to guard myself, but the creature was faster, bigger, and far more adept at swords than I was.

I fell backwards.

The sword came down towards me and I rolled away as I'd watched a hundred fighters do in movies. I didn't drop my shield which made it almost impossible for me to stand up.

I didn't have the dexterity to jump up and stand. I needed a hand behind me to push myself upright.

Vaguely, I heard booing and someone yelling at me to get up.

A moment later, Jeremy was beside me in the arena, a long flaming sword in his hand.

I stared.

The creature continued to hack at me, forcing me to roll from side to side to avoid the slashing sword. It learned my moves. I felt the sting of the sword as it cut my arm again.

Jeremy swung his sword in a high arc, cutting the creature in two from head to pelvis. Fire burned the sides evenly.

Cut in two, each half reformed and turned on Jeremy, two swords flashing to his one flaming one. He held them off, but I could see he was struggling, giving ground.

However, with the creatures distracted, I managed to stand.

Once on my feet, I ran to Jeremy's aid, hacking at one of the creatures, drawing its attention.

Jeremy cut off the head of the creature he faced during its second of distraction.

Then he went after the one I had drawn away. I raised my shield and stepped carefully backwards as it tried to break through my defenses.

When Jeremy got close, ready for another killing blow, it turned to him and while his flaming sword swung through the thing's head, the shadowy skull became an old man's face. The sword the creature swung continued its motion, hacking into Jeremy's arm, drawing a long spurt of blood.

Even as the creature fell, I ran to Jeremy, ripping at my outfit, which turned out to be a white toga that fortunately covered more than Xavier's did, and wrapped it around Jeremy's arm.

He nodded at me, falling to his knees.

"You need to get back to your body," he whispered, breathless.

I looked around for my body.

I saw myself in the middle of the ceremony. Jeremy was down on one knee, head lowered as he continued to chant. Ian stood behind him, holding that rock.

Lauren had rushed up behind Jeremy. I saw her feeding him magical energy. My body was slumped over, lying, a knee drawn up as if I were attempting to kneel on the other side of the tent. With the speed of thought, I appeared before my body.

It looked impossibly small, slumped over , though I knew it wasn't. I squeezed myself inside. The ache of my body, the pain that ripped through me made me not want to continue. But, once again, I forced myself.

Finally, I was fully inside my flesh. I was weak and tired. Opening my eyes to be certain I was really in my body, I noted blood seeping from a wound on one of my arms. It had run down to my fingers and was already drying to a sticky paste.

Whatever I'd fought in that arena had had the ability to hurt me physically.

Jeremy had been badly wounded. My heart leapt to my throat as I looked up, dreading what I might see. Sure enough, blood flowed from his arm, but it was bandaged, though not with white cloth from an imaginary toga. Instead, it looked like a scarf that may once have been white with pink roses on it, but was now pink and red.

Lauren had been the one to bandage Jeremy's arm, sacrificing one of her lovely scarves.

Chapter Twenty-Six

I pushed myself up from the ground. No one seemed to notice me. Xavier was intent upon the group around Rose.

I smelled blood and sweat and realized it was my own body. The rain still poured down, but the wind didn't seem quite as intent upon ripping the tent from the ground.

Breathing deliberately to calm myself, I examined my arm. The sword had cut through my shirt and into my skin, leaving a fairly deep gash in the side of my upper arm. The blood flow had slowed to a light seeping, fortunately.

Over the tingle in my arm, I felt the sting of the wound, as well as a deeper ache that was likely to be with me for some time.

A particularly strong gust of wind lifted the cloth sides of our tent. It swirled about my body making me shiver. I was cold.

The ground beneath my feet felt icy cold though the dirt was dry enough.

My head ached badly. I couldn't wait to take something for the pain. I'd have loved to go back to the clinic and lie down. But if I could be attacked where all the enforcers were, then I could be attacked anywhere. If it hadn't happened here, maybe no one would have noticed that I needed assistance.

The ground shook beneath my feet. Everyone stumbled, working to regain their footing.

A long, low scream of pain echoed through the rain.

The black stallion that had always been the avatar of the heart of the enclave gave a high whinny followed by a loud screech of agony that was abruptly silenced.

The rain stopped.

The ground stopped shaking.

Even the chanting stopped.

Everyone stood completely still, staring straight ahead.

I watched as the old man who had attacked me rose from the ground and moved through Rose, the way a ghost in a movie might. He made no move to possess her, but merely stepped through her. Then he stood beside her, dressed in brown clothing from another era, the frayed edges of his jacket attesting to the fact that he hadn't been a rich man.

He walked in front of each of the people involved in the re-dedication, looking each in the eye. He slapped Elena across the cheek. He spit on Jeanine. Bernice he punched, but she stood straight despite the impact. I wondered if she was that strong or if the punch hadn't hurt the way it looked. He kicked Randi. When he reached Jeremy he pressed his fingers against the wound, whispering something.

I watched as Jeremy's bright golden magical threads leaked out much like blood, draining to the ground.

In the silence, he groaned.

Then Ambrose, because that's who it had to have been, was gone.

I heard another whinny, this one softer, more uncertain.

Rose gasped and sat up. Her head tilted back at the tent covering, surprise spreading across her face. Her body hung in that position for an agonizing second before she fell back against the bed, hard. If I'd had the energy, I'd have been tempted to go to her.

The ground began to rumble and shake. I sank to my knees, my fingers grasping at the dirt as if that could steady me. I didn't know how anyone continued to stand, though most who did so held onto something. Ian looked a little green, as if he were about to vomit.

Thunder cracked above our heads, so loud I thought lightning had hit the tent. Nothing burned and I didn't feel a jolt of electricity. Of course, I hurt so badly all over that another jolt probably wouldn't have mattered.

Another cry from the stallion, but this one stronger, angrier. Wind whistled around the tent in every direction. This must be what it felt like to be in the center of a tornado. Rain splattered on the roof. Although Lauren had created a regular wooden roof, not cloth, it sank in the middle.

I looked up at the others. Lauren had slumped against Jeremy, her eyes closed. She looked as if she were in pain.

Jeremy looked as if he were barely hanging on. While magic was being fed into what looked like a colorful vortex around Rose, I noted that nearly nothing was being fed from Jeremy, despite Lauren's assistance.

I pushed myself up.

The ground shook again. I stumbled to the side, nearly crashing into Randi.

I was thankful I had avoided hitting her, certain that to break her concentration would be to destroy the re-dedication.

Another step, although my feet seemed too heavy to lift. The ground shook once more as if the very act of my walking was making the earth tremble. I am a big woman, but I am not that big. I managed to stay upright, but only just.

I held my arm close to my body, cradling it. I heard the wind and the soft chants that surrounded me once again.

I made it another two steps before the ground shook, harder this time.

Swaying to the side, I threw my arms out to keep from falling. I brushed Jeanine's back but she didn't turn, didn't look at me.

I made it to Jeremy and placed a hand on him, turning on the faucet as Win had taught me and let him take magic from me. My eyes drifted shut, though this time I didn't see the magical colors.

The sounds of the wind died away. The earth stopped shuddering every few seconds.

Finally, I heard a final breath and then silence, once again.

I kept my eyes closed, not wanting to look around and see that there was more work to be done.

I no longer felt the magic pouring from me. I still had reserves. I hadn't been drained. I felt Jeremy sag to the ground. Something heavy pressed against my head.

That forced me to open my eyes, to see what was happening. Lauren had passed out, or worse, her body leaning against mine.

Ian had slumped also and now sat cross-legged on the ground, head down. Jeremy wasn't conscious, though I felt him breathing.

Win was helping Ian. Next to me, Jeanine sat, head in her hand, eyes closed. Randi slumped next to her. Bernice lay on the ground, face up to the sky, taking deep breaths as if she'd run miles. Elena knelt on the ground, leaning forward like she was about to move into a yoga pose.

Over in the back, where I'd been, Xavier leaned over from a standing position, hands on knees, drawing in deep breaths. His hands shook slightly as he pushed himself up.

Finally, I looked at Rose, or rather where Rose had been. Nothing remained, not even the bed.

Although it continued to rain, the building crumbled around us. I braced, expecting it to fall on me, but it just disappeared. We were a sorry group of people laying around on the wet ground in the rain, although the storm was passing. There wasn't even much wind.

Nearby the black stallion walked over. Now, instead of being all black he had a large white chevron on his nose. He walked carefully, almost fearful of approaching us. When he got to Ian, he nudged him with his nose. Ian reached out and rubbed him. The stallion stood taller and looked over at us.

A number of creatures, a few rabbits, two cats, one large black one that I thought was Ian's Socrates, along with my Peony, and a Harlequin Great Dane all padded up to us, encircling us as we'd encircled Rose a little bit ago.

Large crows, or more accurately, ravens joined them. First two, then four more, then perhaps a dozen more, all landed around us and watched. One of the ravens glided down and sat on Lauren's back.

She didn't move. Another landed on Jeremy. He also didn't move.

I pulled away, suddenly fearful that I was cuddling with two dead bodies. I wiped the rain drops from my face and took a longer look at them. Lauren's chest rose, but her breathing was shallow and slow. She was alive, barely.

I couldn't tell if Jeremy was still with us. I'd felt him

breathing earlier, or maybe I'd confused his breath with Lauren's.

Another raven landed on him. The two birds hopped around and cawed, apparently at each other. One bent down and made a loud caw sound in his ear. Jeremy shuddered. Then his chest began to rise and fall once again, though like Lauren, it was shallow and slow.

The birds stayed there, settling on them. The other ravens watched.

In the distance, I heard a golf cart. I tried to remember who was around to rescue us, to take us to the clinic. We had Gretchen and Katrina watching Gerald. David was watching Lucas.

I didn't have to wonder long. Dr. Mulrooney drove up in the golf cart and looked around at us, shaking her head.

"Anyone who can walk, get to the clinic," she ordered. Win took Ian's arm and guided him through the grass, her rollator going slowly but able to plow through the greenery. Ian stumbled along. Win wasn't much better, but her rollator allowed her to stay upright.

Cassandra appeared from between shrubbery, hurrying along.

"First time I've ever gotten a call from a shadow cat," she said. "It just appeared on the wall and said we had to get out here. Now."

"Jeremy and Lauren are the worst," Bernice whispered, her voice hoarse as if instead of chanting she'd been screaming for the last hour or so.

Dr. Mulrooney came over to where I sat, doing a quick examination of both Lauren and Jeremy. She shook her head at both of them and noticed the blood on Jeremy's arm.

My arms began to tingle, although they were so achy and sore from the magic that had been going on, the tingling felt as if my arms were finally waking after going numb. The sensation felt distant.

I moved a bit further back as Dr. Mulrooney worked. Cassandra came over and opened the first aid kit, pulling out items. They pulled the scarf from Jeremy's arm. Only then did I see just how deep the gash went. I turned away.

The two worked on him for a while before using a magical stretcher to take him over to the golf cart. Then they went to work on Lauren, who needed less, but definitely had to be carried to the cart.

Dr. Mulrooney got in and drove off. Cassandra checked other people out, looking at eyes and checking breathing. She made me get up and sit in the other golf cart, the one that Rose had driven. She put Elena in the cart and also Randi who looked particularly pale.

"I'll be back for the rest of you, if you can't walk," she said quietly as she drove off. I barely kept my eyes open for the short drive.

Chapter Twenty-Seven

Just that morning, I'd been in a clinic bed thankful I was there for safety and not because I was injured. And now, only a few hours later, I was back in the same bed, because, once again, I was hurt.

My arm was bandaged. According to Cassandra who did the suturing, I needed three stitches and chances were there'd be a scar, although there were people on the island who could take care of that.

Jeremy was still out. His wound had required far more sutures than mine. Cassandra didn't want to say much more about anyone else, keeping everyone's condition private.

Lauren still wasn't awake, though Cassandra thought I might be able to speak to her before the day was out. I hoped that Jeremy woke before then, even if I wasn't able to speak with him.

I stank of mud and dirt. While my stomach growled and I needed food, I also wanted to clean up. According to Cassandra, I'd have to shower with my arm out the door for the next week or so, until the sutures dissolved. I was to come in daily and have them checked.

Ian shuffled into my room. Win wasn't with him.

"She's at the B&B, cleaning house, so to speak. Lucas did have something come up, but David was prepared. He had locked Lucas in a room, alone. Win made sure it was possible. David put up a protection spell around the room and the creature inside. Lucas, however, is exhausted, as it seems trying to get out of the room used up a lot of his magic. He'll be leaving on the next ferry which comes in a few hours."

"I don't hear rain any longer," I said.

"It's a gorgeous afternoon. I checked my phone to see what the forecasters are saying and they can't explain it. I guess the storm settled over the entire area from Milwaukee to Muskegon," Ian said.

He sighed, looking around for a chair.

"I still feel drugged out. The island feels different. Gentler, as if it's pushing me gently from behind to do certain things I've been putting off. It's not ignoring me, not that the island really ignored me, but before it left me much more to my own choices. Now I have a sense of what it wants from me."

"Was Rose like that? I didn't know her."

Ian cocked his head, eyes on the scenery, mostly trees, outside. "I didn't know her well, but she did sort of mother Xavier. It's going to take some getting used to, not having her at the station. She was old and slow, but she had power and presence, you know?"

I nodded.

"I guess I can see her mothering me now. I mean, she worked with Xavier and now she works with me…" Ian trailed off and then lifted his arms in a who knows gesture.

Cassandra arrived with a cart of food, which could

have fed half the island but it was for me and probably Ian.

"Is Derry's back to normal?" I asked when Cassandra left, walking a bit more slowly than usual.

"Of course," Ian said. "Win went over there to make sure. Bernice, Carl, and Xavier said they'd seen enough of the clinic and have set up camp, as Win put it, at Derry's, eating their way through everything they can."

"And the others?" I asked.

"Everyone is good except Jeremy and Lauren. I think they expect that Lauren will wake up soon enough, but Dr. Mulrooney has some concerns about Jeremy. Fortunately, Blake, one of the enforcers waiting for it to be safe for the ferry, has some healing magic. He's often the medic if someone gets hurt on an assignment. We're hoping he can help out. It's not as if Dr. Mulrooney and Cassandra haven't been pushed to their limits. I've seen the piles of food coming in, and it's not just for all of us."

I'd already eaten, though I felt as if I could eat again. I picked my way through my favorites before deciding to give my stomach a rest. I still drank some more orange juice. Plenty of calories without taking up as much space in my stomach.

I continued to talk to Ian for a bit before my eyelids drooped. Ian took that as a sign that he needed to leave. I wondered vaguely if he were going back to the B&B or if he was staying at the clinic.

Chapter Twenty-Eight

Two days later, I was recovering at home. Tulip was cuddlier than normal and Peony seemed bossier, but that could have been my imagination. I wondered how much the changeover affected them. They were magic, so they were linked to the heart in some way.

I walked up to the B&B to see Ian, who had mostly recovered. Elena and Jeanine had left. I missed out on the six enforcers who came to the island to check things out, smooth over any rough edges, and to remove and examine Lucas, Gerald, and Grant.

Lucas was being treated. Gerald would be going to Far Haven, the prison enclave for mages. Apparently, he wasn't simply influenced, or if he was, he wasn't willing to let go of it.

Grant would have to go through any number of examinations and processes to make sure he was no longer influenced. He'd also be unable to do the job he'd always done. My understanding from Ian was that once you'd been influenced, it was much easier for it to happen again.

Jack was still recovering in a hospital from his time in a boat on the lake. He'd used up nearly all of his magic to remain afloat and had been fortunate that the current had dragged him near the shore where one of our mages had been out looking for people and picked him up. He was treated mundanely for exposure and magically for overuse of magic. Having been examined, they found he'd been influenced, but wasn't actively a part of the attempt to overthrow the island.

Naturally, Jack was horrified when he found out what he'd done… again. And being Jack, he couldn't live with that. He resigned from the accounting office, sent a long apology to me via email, and sent someone to pick up his things. He planned to live in the ordinary world where he believed he'd be safer from influence and less of a danger to others.

Win remained behind to continue teaching Ian, although with Rose as the heart, he was learning faster than he had before. He got regular prods from the island.

Jeremy was still in the hospital, though I was told he'd woken briefly and gone back to sleep. Several muscles in his arm had been completely severed. While magic could help heal those in a way that ordinary medicine might not, it was going to be a long haul before he was better. The magic I'd seen the former heart take from him was gone for good, no matter how much he accepted himself. Rumor had it, he'd be looking for a new job.

I walked slowly out of my home and up to the B&B to see Ian and perhaps have breakfast with him. Food was a huge part of my recovery.

The B&B looked brighter than it had in a long time, perhaps ever. I couldn't quite put my finger on how, but it was like changing the light on a camera setting. The colors seemed to sparkle. Some of the flowers blooming offered sweet smells as I walked up the short path. The Japanese maple waved it leaves in the light breeze.

The sun was out, although a light breeze kept the morning from feeling warm. The three cats, one black, one white, one orange tabby, snoozed under the maple. They glanced at me as I walked through. The black one yawned when I met its gaze, as if bored by my presence.

I climbed the stairs and opened the door. Inside, like the outside, seemed brighter and shinier than before. The floors weren't just clean, they gleamed and shone. The paint looked fresher. I smelled the faintest hint of new paint beneath the wonderful scents of food and coffee that wafted from the dining area.

It wasn't Eggs Benedict morning, but I wanted a big breakfast. Plus, I wanted to see Ian again. Dirk and Bill were at a table near the window. I wondered when they had arrived back. I'd heard Sandra, my neighbor coming in the evening before, but I hadn't gone out to welcome her home. I couldn't blame her for leaving, but it seemed to me that she'd taken the easy way out. I'd stayed and fought for the island. Not that I'd been given a choice.

Lauren sat at a table by herself. She smiled when she saw me and waved me over. I joined her, looking at the food.

Those of us who had fought had all suffered major changes in our lives—jobs lost, a life lost, coworkers gone.

Ian sashayed out in his usual style. Today he wore gray trousers that showed off his bare ankles. He had on navy blue sneakers with low socks peeking out, probably to protect his heels from rubbing against the back of the shoes. Today's vest was a bright blue and green plaid and he'd added a gray bowtie to his white shirt.

"Fancy," I said.

He touched it and smiled. "Win said it would be perfect to pull the outfit together. I wanted a brighter look to match the B&B's new sparkle, you know?"

"It suits you," I told him, which made him beam.

"I heard Jeremy is getting out of the hospital," Ian said, keeping his voice low. "And he'll be staying here. I think Cassandra is bringing him over in the next hour."

"How's he doing?" I asked.

"Rumor has it, he's grumpy, but then again that's a safe bet. He was always a little grumpy. And I'd be grumpy, too, if I lost my job. Heck, I don't have a clue what I'd have done if we'd lost the enclave and I wasn't the Innkeeper any longer."

I nodded, thinking. I was lucky. My job was fairly ordinary. I worked with numbers and did accounting. There were plenty of places I could do that. I just happened to like the people on Jewel.

Lauren sipped her tea. "I wouldn't know what to do if I weren't the librarian."

"I'm so glad you're okay," I told her. Once again, she'd been the one to get injured and bravely pushed herself through it. In comparison my injuries always seemed lesser. I hoped that if I'd been in her shoes, I'd have been as resilient.

"I just over did it a little," Lauren said. "Nothing you haven't done before."

Ian rolled his eyes and shook his head, pointing at Lauren, as if to say she'd been more injured than she let on.

After Ian gave me today's choices, I ordered the waffles with a side of sausages and more coffee. I was still eating more than usual but I was no longer famished all the time.

When Dirk and Bill left, Ian joined me and Lauren at the table. Win wandered in with her rollator and the table, which had been a square two-top became a rectangular four top. She settled in a chair with her rollator behind her.

"You look better," she said, nodding at me before turning to Lauren. "And you are starting to look yourself again."

Lauren gave her a small smile. She did look paler than she had. The scarf she wore was plainer than usual, light blue with white swirls. I had thought it was the colors that made her seem pale, but perhaps not.

"The B&B looks stunning. Is that the new heart or just you?" I asked Ian.

"That's Rose," Ian said. "She likes me. Like I said, she's sort of motherly and she's shining things up around here. I love it. There are brighter colors in the rooms, too, and less floral wallpaper. Now it's much more modern looking, but still comfortable."

I laughed. The floral wallpaper had not really been Ian's style.

"Oh thank God!" Lauren said. "I hated that wallpaper. And the clashing rugs! I wondered why you chose that for us."

Ian just smiled a cat-like smile, not willing to say a word.

"I went into work, but not much had changed in the office. Bernice helped me put out a notice for a bookkeeper," I said. "At least it's not tax time or something horrible, although I could probably get Jack to work remotely in a pinch. He doesn't even want to do that, right now. He wants to stay as far away from here as he can. I hope he doesn't blame me."

"It's Jack," Ian said. "He probably blames himself and

is embarrassed. And he probably worries about doing more damage."

"Should I press him to at least work remotely?" I asked.

Win shook her head. "That's part of who Jack is. Our job is to accept him. At least that's how I like to think about it."

"But I'd like to support him and let him know we don't blame him."

"He's been told that a million times, but he doesn't believe it," Win said gently. "Besides, the heart wanted you. I suspect there might be triggers that go off if Jack spends too much time with you. While working remote would make it impossible for him to influence you negatively, it could cause him problems in the ordinary world."

I could accept that. Jack would hate causing more trouble.

Lauren and I ate while Ian and Win sipped coffee.

Finishing, I heard the door open. Ian was up in a second, hurrying over to greet the newcomer.

I turned to see Cassandra helping Jeremy inside. He'd lost weight, leaving hollows in his cheeks. His arm was in a sling with so many bandages I couldn't tell whether or not it was in a cast. The pants he wore hung on him. David could fix that soon enough, but Jeremy would have to have the energy to take them to David's shop.

"I have the perfect room for you," Ian said, hurrying over to him, letting Jeremy lean on his arm instead of Cassandra's.

Jeremy looked around. He met my eyes and gave a small smile.

"I'd love some breakfast if it's still going on," he said.

Win stood, pointed her rollator to the back of the room, and took her leave.

"Naturally," Ian said. "Holly and Lauren are just

finishing, but I'll keep refilling their coffee cups so they'll stick around to keep you company."

Ian winked at me from behind Jeremy.

Lauren caught the look and smiled, something that reminded of me of Ian's knowing smile. "I really need to get back to the library," she said. "Sorry, Jeremy. I'm glad to see you're doing better, though."

"Thanks," he said sitting down across from me.

I couldn't help the way my heart fluttered. Despite how worn he looked, he was still attractive. I waved at Lauren, who just kept on smiling, bigger than I would have expected from someone not quite recovered.

"You look as if you did okay. And only a scratch from the sword," he said.

"I haven't had a chance to thank you for saving my life in the arena, or whatever that place was," I said.

"The heart pulled it from your subconscious. You handled yourself well. Xavier reported that you fought off the heart exceptionally well. He noticed no influencing, although whoever replaces Grant will probably have to examine you just to be sure."

Ian brought coffee, refilling my cup as promised and pouring some for Jeremy. I took cream, no sugar. Jeremy drank his black.

"Waffles or eggs?" Ian asked.

"Both?" Jeremy asked.

Ian gave him a quick nod and sashayed off.

Jeremy shook his head. "It must be nice to move so easily. I never realized all the things I took for granted until this."

"What will you do now?" I asked, hoping I wasn't being too nosy.

"Heal," he said. "And think about what other things I might do. It's all up in the air right now. At least the U council will pay for me to stay here as long as I want while I figure that out."

I sipped my coffee to hide a smile. Ian was doing a little circle dance in the doorway of the kitchen. At least until Win grabbed him and pulled him away.

Things were definitely looking up around Jewel Island.

About Bonnie Elizabeth

Bonnie Elizabeth could never decide what to do, so she wrote stories about amazing things and sometimes she even finished them.

While rejection stung her so badly in person, she spent most of her young life talking to cats and dogs rather than people, she was unusually resilient when it came to rejections on her writing, racking up a good number of them.

Floating through a variety of jobs, including veterinary receptionist, cemetery administrator, and finally acupuncturist, she continued to write stories.

When the internet came along (yes she's old), she started blogging as her cat, because we all know cats don't notice rejection. Then she started publishing.

Bonnie writes in a variety of genres. Her popular Whisper series is contemporary fantasy and her Teenage Fairy Godmother series is written for teens. She has been published in a number of anthologies and is working on expanding her writing repertoire.

She lives with her husband (who talks less than she does) and her three cats, who always talk back.

Find her at www.bonnielizabeth.com

Stay in Touch

Also by Bonnie Elizabeth

The Frost Witch Saga

October Snow

November Frost

December Storm

Familiar Cafe Series

Unfamiliar Magic

Unfair Magic

Appalachian Souls

Souls Lost

Souls Broken

The Ash Jericho Series

An Inheritance to Die For

A Discovery to Die For

A Distraction to Die For

The Whisper Novels

Whisper Bound

Taken by the Sound

An Air of Suspicion

Little Dog Lost

Death Interrupted

Down in Whisper

A Haunting Whisper

A Haunting Attraction

Secrets Not Whispers

Only Human

Other Novels

One Bad Wish

Sun Spot Magic

Ghosts from the Past

Unnatural Secrets

Shadows of Solstice

The Haunting of Steely Woods

Find them all at your favorite bookseller or check us out at
MyBigFatOrangeCat.com

www.ingramcontent.com/pod-product-compliance
Lightning Source LLC
Chambersburg PA
CBHW032223190726
48289CB00007BA/2366